**LINKERS: Book 1 – Chickee**

A Mother's Heart Beat

A double lifetime of love and loss and helping others

KATHY ARMSTRONG PUDIL

A Mother's Heart Beat (Linkers: Book 1 – Chickee)
Copyright 2021: Kathy Armstrong Pudil
ISBN-13: 9798754581265
All rights reserved.

Cover Design & Formatting: Laura Shinn Designs
http://laurashinn.yolasite.com

Dedication

To all those who have a mother's heart: loving, giving, sacrificing, healing. Even if you don't have your own children, you still have a heart for loving and helping others.

And especially to my mother, Lexie Armstrong, whom I love and admire so much. Her heartbeat calms mine.

~ * ~ * ~ * ~

A Mother's Heartbeat

A Mother's Heart Beat. A mother's heartbeat walks around outside her body, making dangerous and risky moves without her permission. How could Chickee ever become a mom if it was so dangerous and painful?

Table of Contents

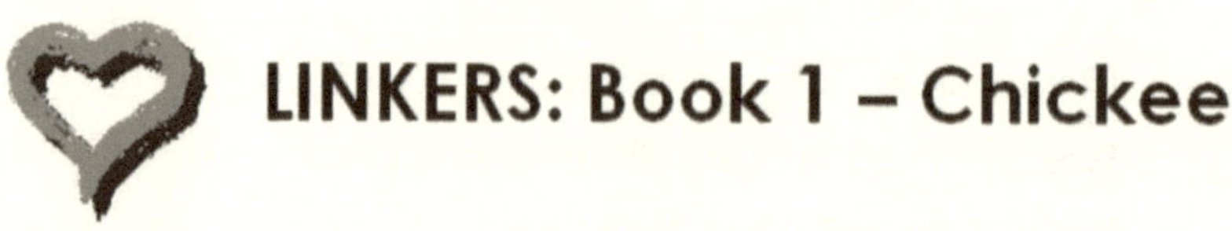

A Mother's Heart Beat

Chapter One

Remembering

April 2092

She sat there with a tear trickling down her cheek.

"What's the matter, Chickee?" asked the nurse's aide who passed out napkins and tableware.

"I was just remembering...." she answered. "Sometimes when I hear my own heartbeat, I remember things."

Chickee usually took pride in her upbeat attitude, but today was a hard day. A flood of memories swirled around in her head, and it seemed that the sad ones came to the surface today. Her mind skipped to the moment she decided to create Mother's Heartbeat.

2012

He was twelve years old. His name was Todd. He had leukemia and his mother had died two years earlier in a horrendous car accident where a semi-truck ran over her car on the Interstate. He found out he had the leukemia only six weeks after burying his mom.

Chickee was good friends with Teresa, his mother. Chickee and Jared kept in touch with Todd's grandparents, and helped out in Todd's care when they could. She took a shift twice a week to sit with Todd in the hospital so his grandma could run errands and have some time to herself. His grandparents had plans to adopt Todd. It seemed like the daily toll of treatments, reactions to medicines, and hospitalizations got in the way of all the other important things of life. But Todd was a fighter. To Chickee's delight, Todd enjoyed her visits immensely, because she reminded him of his real mom. Having her there was about as close as having his mom back as he could get.

Chickee held, cradled this small, sick twelve-year-old boy whose heart was "listening" to her heartbeat. She got a stethoscope for this purpose, because it seemed to really make a difference in Todd's recovery when he went on a downhill turn like this one. His head rested weakly on her shoulder. Suddenly it came to her: a technological device that helps connect one person's heartbeat to another's heartbeat rhythm. Sending a body's memory back to the nurturing and safe haven of the womb. Prenatal communication of swish-swish and tha-thump, tha-thump.

Back in the eighties, people caught on to the idea of sound as a catalyst for change. Truthfully, the recognition of the power of sound to impact a person's healing ability happened many years before. People used "positive energy" techniques long before Mother's Heartbeat was even an idea in Chickee's mind. Family members of patients who were in a coma were encouraged to speak to their loved ones, because the belief was that they could hear, even if they couldn't respond or indicate in any way that they knew what the person was saying to them.

Nurse Tara passed around the iced tea. Only it didn't have ice in it. That always bugged Chickee, but she never told anyone. The lady who sat next to her at mealtimes rolled into place at the table and set the brake on her hover chair.

"What are you looking at?"

Chickee looked away. She often wondered why so many of the residents were in a bad mood all the time. She wiped away her tears defiantly and took a sip of lukewarm tea, wondering what would be served for dinner tonight. Murphy, over at the next table, smiled and waved at her, flirtatious as ever. She nodded her head at him. He constantly flirted with all the ladies in Green Valley.

Her mind wandered again into the past. She thought about her best friend, Stella. Having known each other for over half their lives, she and Stella were friends through thick and thin. One of the things that always stuck out in Chickee's mind as she reminisced about their friendship was the times they went and helped on disaster relief efforts, first for Hurricane Katrina in 2005, and again when the Joplin tornado hit in 2011. Those selfless exhausting times were the ones when you see a person's true colors, and Chickee knew she and Stella had kindred hearts for helping people. It was a lot of hard work, clearing debris, passing out drinking water, organizing places for people to stay while their homes and neighborhoods were being rebuilt. All of it required selfless and determined people with a vision for making the world a better place. She also knew how much of a gem Lee was for supporting Stella and her in their determination to help people. Although Chickee didn't have a child in those years, Stella relied upon Lee to watch a five-year-old Tommy while she answered the call to assist. If only Chickee had the energy now to help people in a real and meaningful way.

James and Tara slowly passed around trays of food to the residents. The guy with hair going in every direction yelled loudly. He was always angry. When James set the tray of food down in front of Wild Hair, he flipped it over onto the floor. "I guess you're not hungry today, Pete?" James asked him.

Chickee went back into her own thoughts. Todd had completed seven rounds of chemotherapy when she went in to link heartbeats with him. He was so weak; the doctors were concerned he would give up. Chickee was determined to not let that happen. She focused on the connection and tried to clear her mind of everything except the heartbeat and the healing thoughts.

She also believed in the power of prayer. Sometimes she felt like her work as a Mother's Heartbeat Rep was as much a prayer warrior's job as anything. When sickness and pain make a person feel powerless, sometimes the only thing left to do is pray.

She needed put all these memories to sleep for awhile, or she would start crying again. Tara set a tray of *white and yellow* in front of Chickee. Some kind of white meat about the size of the palm of her hand. White gravy on top of white mashed (boxed) potatoes, yellow corn kernels in a small pile going astray into the potatoes, and a white Styrofoam cup of white pear slices. She smiled to herself remembering how, as a kid, she would argue Skittles are a balanced meal, because they "make a colorful plate" like the health class book said. "Aim to serve a meal that has a variety of color. A colorful plate is not only appealing to the eye, but most likely to address all five food groups." Ha. She could make a colorful plate without any white foods; just give her a bag of Skittles. She reluctantly dug her fork into the white mound of potatoes with gravy.

If she knew then what she knew now, would she still have been a Mother's Heartbeat Rep?

Chapter Two

No Regrets

2014

The excruciating headaches were something Chickee had at first chalked up to stress when she started linking with Todd. But no doubt about it, longevity meant she could continue to help people. Continuing to help people meant longevity. And the headaches were something Chickee had gotten used to over the years. When the idea for linking heartbeats first occurred to Chickee, she sat down to do some research. She knew whenever she talked to her mother over the phone, hearing Mom's voice soothed her troubles and sent her racing heartbeat down a notch, but was there any research on heartbeats "hearing" each other?

Studies showed people who focus on a common activity in unison often maintain the same cadence of heartbeat. One study Chickee found revealed people who sing together in a choir actually align their heartbeats as they sing together. The evidence was there. Heartbeats "listen" to one another.

Todd seemed to visibly relax. As he rested with the stethoscope earbuds tucked into his ears, she focused on calm, pleasant, healing thoughts. She knew a bit about herbal remedies, so her first inclination was to imagine the herbs that cause relaxation: chamomile, with its small yellow, puffy blooms; valerian root and its pungent rooty smell; hyssop, purple fuzzy pods of healing and calming in them; also purple and calming: lavender and sage.

For a moment, she was distracted by the people out in the hallway of the hospital, wailing and crying. People with their own various family or friends to visit. Several crying teenagers came out of a room across the hall. Chickee remembered the newscast from last night--two local teens very seriously injured in a car accident; the driver, under the influence of alcohol. From the looks of the waiting room when she walked through, several of their friends were holding a vigil for the two who were in critical condition. She wondered if any of those kids had someone to link and listen to heartbeats with for comfort and healing. Returning to her own task, she refocused on Todd or she would be sending him the wrong signals.

She stayed with him, connected at least by touch of a hand or her palm resting on his arm until he was breathing deeply again. She was stiff. She needed to stretch, and get a drink of water. As she stood, she realized she had a horrible throbbing headache. The fluorescent lights in the hospital hallway were painfully bright. The pounding in her head was nearly unbearable.

It was the first headache of many. Every linking session caused the Linker to have a horrible headache after treatment. That was the price paid for being a Linker.

Chickee headed towards the cafeteria and bought a water and an orange. She sat down near a window, even though it seemed like a black night on the other side of the glass, and she peeled the orange by first ripping the two ends off, then tearing strips of rind off until the full, whole orange was a juicy ball waiting to be sectioned and slurped.

She carefully laid out a napkin and set the peeled orange down on it. It made a wet circle on the paper napkin. Without even wiping the stickiness off her fingers, she cradled her head between her palms and prayed for her headache to subside. Next, she sectioned the orange, and ate it sliver by sliver, peeling off the stringy whites before popping them into her mouth. She ignored her headache. She thought more about the concept of making this a real opportunity for helping others. What would it take? How does a person begin a project like this? She would have to ask Joan—after her head quit hurting and she'd had a chance to rest, and of course checked on Todd again.

Chapter Three

Mother's Heartbeat Grows

2014

Chickee wondered if there was a mom next door who could be a heartbeat link for that child, too. Moms were always the best candidates for being a child's heartbeat Linker. It's the most soothing heartbeat a person knows--from prenatal memory. Funny how Chickee's non-mother heartbeat is equally as soothing as the real mom heartbeat, as long as she links and focuses on the positive images and messages. "Send the love," said her first Mother's Heartbeat recruit Linker, Rana.

Rana was a *real* mom. She lost her second child as a newborn to a mysterious virus that swept through the neo-natal ICU in 2013. She also had a three-year-old boy named Mikey. Chickee had recently developed her idea and asked Jared to create the Velcro wrist wrap version of the linking system. Rana felt like she needed to do something to honor the memory of her sweet Hannah. When Chickee approached her about becoming a Linker and trying the new system out, she immediately wanted to become a volunteer heartbeat Linker for sick children. She specifically wanted to serve kids who had lost a mom, feeling like the link would be a completion—like two puzzle pieces fitting together—her as a mom who lost a child, and the child who lost a mom.

Mother's Heartbeat started out as a community service for those whose moms had either died or were unavailable or unknown. As knowledge and success of efforts grew, Chickee aimed to make Mother's Heartbeat a non-profit organization. She didn't leave her teaching career until she was able to pull comparable income from the organization as she did from being in school nine months out of the year. The first two years, when she taught full time and worked to increase the load and number of Linkers working to link with hospitalized children, it was amazing she didn't lose her mind. She prayed her teaching didn't suffer too badly; she knew her heart had turned from teaching to linking, and things would never be the same.

Through the Mother's Heartbeat non-profit organization, Chickee developed an entire network of moms who had lost children to connect with children without moms for hospital emergencies and chronic situations. The goal was to set up a system that insured if, in the event of a childhood emergency, a young person would already be on the list to link for healing. Very quickly, the research and data showed children who linked with a Linker for the first three days after their injury, surgery, or emergency were twice as likely to experience a full recovery as those who did not experience linking with a Mother's Heartbeat Linker.

After Tommy's accident in the barn fire, the choice to become a Linker was a natural step for Stella. She wanted to help the moms who felt so helpless as they watched their sick child in the hospital. She took to linking like a fish to water. Stella was often inclined to take the cases of older children and young teens. She also became Chickee's greatest promoter and advocate to recruit new Linkers. Stella became one of the most active and reliable Linkers Chickee had. Their bond of friendship seemed to become even closer as they both strived for the common goal of filling a need in the lives of sick children.

Chapter Four

A Shepherd's Heart Breaks

2014

Chickee was driving down the road on a spring afternoon. The trees were starting to bud, and the daffodil blooms were bowing heavy, bright yellow heads down to the ground. Up ahead in the distance, she noticed a huge plume of dark gray smoke. It seemed to be right around her friend Stella's farmhouse. It could be evidence of a large brush pile burning, but the smoke seemed too dark. Stella and her husband Lee had raised sheep there for at least seventeen years. Their son, Tommy helped with the chores ever since he was barely old enough to walk. He loved the sheep herder's life as much as his dad did. It seemed a very difficult and strenuous life to Chickee, but they loved it.

They had two barns. One was for wintering the flocks, and one was for storing hay, grain and equipment. Their farmhouse was about one hundred yards north of the winter barn, and was a traditional style Civil War era farmhouse. Stella and Lee and made some really nice upgrades in the home, so it suited them perfectly. To Chickee, the kitchen seemed small, even though they had completely remodeled and upgraded it to dark granite countertops and beautiful Spanish tile floors.

They had done some really neat things with Tommy's loft room as well. It was mostly enclosed and the wooden beams were exposed along the ceiling. Single bare light bulbs hung down on pendants of various length, and gave the room an industrial feel. One wall of his room was lined with metal sheeting, and had become a magnetic board for all his many artistic efforts. And Tommy was quite an artist. He had an eye for the unusual and unique. He saw details others didn't, and when he drew them out exaggerated, it created a dreamlike sense of artistic flair.

As Chickee drove closer to the farm, she suspected the worst. The smoke plume was too large and too dark to simply be a controlled brush fire. Then she heard the sirens. *Oh dear.* She knew she needed to stop. Although she wasn't sure how she could help. She dialed the hospital and told them she would have to cancel her appointment for linking today. She knew she could call Jared later, after she figured out what the situation was here.

As she drove down the gravel driveway, she saw how much was consumed in fire and flame and she didn't have any words. She saw Stella on the ground, on her knees with her hands pulling on her hair. As Chickee stopped the car, she parked off to the side and rushed across the gravel, over to her friend. She stood beside her, kneeling down and putting her hand on Stella's shoulder. Tears pricked at the corners of her eyes. "Stella? Lee? Are you guys okay? Where's Tommy?" Her own voice sounded frantic, like it belonged to somebody else. The sirens continually wailed louder as the fire truck turned into their driveway.

Stella didn't even look at her. Instead, she rocked back and forth on her knees, her arms wrapped around her body and a grief stricken look of disbelief on her face. It looked like she was trying to keep herself together. She breathed in short, hiccupping gasps of air. She tried to answer Chickee, but the most heart-wrenching wail of grief was all that escaped her lips. She just held on and rocked herself while Chickee assessed the situation.

"Tommy? He's in there? Oh no! No! No!" Stella confirmed Chickee's suspicions with a nod of her head. "Oh Stella!" Chickee pulled her friend's rocking body closer, and put an arm around her.

The fire truck pulled up close as it could to the burning winter barn, and several firemen jumped out as the big rig slowed to a stop. They flung open the hatches, pulled out lengths of hose, and rushed to tame the fire. "Is there anyone inside?" one fireman asked them with urgency.

"Our son, Tommy! He rushed in to save several ewes with their lambs..." Lee was standing behind Stella and Chickee. She saw he had the same stricken look on his face as Stella; but at least he found words to communicate the facts. "We tried to talk him out of it, but he ran in there before we could stop him! It's been too long. It's too late. He's been in there too long.... TOMMY!" Lee crumpled to his knees and put his head in his hands as he sobbed.

Stella seemed in a daze. Chickee was at a loss for words. She stayed there with her arm around Stella's shoulder as they both knelt in the grass and watched the dark smoke billow toward the sky. The crackle of the fire wafted all sorts of sickly smells outward. The two women knelt there in shock. Tears streamed down their faces, staring at the flames as if it was all an unbelievable bad dream and soon they were going to wake up.

The firemen showered the barn with streams of water, trying to quench the orange and yellow tongues of flame lapping up the winter barn, the paint, the boards, and shingles. Chickee and Stella watched the black billows break intermittently as the water cut through the smoke.

Suddenly, they saw a yellow clad fireman come out of the left side of the barn with a bundle in his arms. Tommy was limp and dripping black drops of smoky water. At the fire truck, the fireman laid him down gently and began assessing his injuries. As she stood back and watched Stella run to his side, Chickee silently prayed, *God, please let him be all right.*

Tommy coughed and sputtered, then let out a raspy, "Mom?"

"I'm right here, baby. You're going to be okay. Mom is here. Let these nice men help you. I'm not leaving. I'm right here," Stella sobbed through the words she spoke.

Chickee released a huge breath, not even aware that she had been holding it, waiting to see if he was okay. *Thank you, God, oh, thank you!* She went over to where he lay on the ground. The fireman wrapped up the angry burn all along Tommy's right shoulder, arm and hand. Chickee grabbed his other hand and attempted to link with him directly to ease his pain, to help him heal.

Lee had composed himself momentarily and was sitting on the porch of the farm house, his head in his hands, his elbows on his knees. It looked to Chickee like he was fervently praying the firemen could get the flames under control before they spread to the south barn. She was thankful the wind was almost nonexistent today, or the monster would have licked up the farmhouse and south barn as well. Chickee imagined the numbers running through Lee's head. Even worse, he was remembering the sweet personalities of his lost ewes. And at least seven precious lambs lost, too. Now he knew his son was alive, she clearly saw that the shepherd's heart was breaking for his lost sheep.

This whole day, the clock seemed to stand still. By the time dusk arrived, Lee, Jared, and Chickee were exhausted and numb. Too much emotion for one day. Chickee had called Jared, and when he got off work, he thoughtfully brought out a bucket of chicken and some biscuits. None of them were very hungry, though, so they offered the meal to the firefighters as they packed up their truck and hoses.

It seemed like such a loss. A loss of life; a loss of wealth; but ironically, no loss of words for Lee. "Darla, the most matronly and consistent ewe was, at least, out in the field with her new lamb. But Coffee, Teek, and WL!" He cringed as his face screwed up tightly trying to hold back the tears. "All three girls, lost! And Fluffy! And that new lamb of Teek's, so unusually small and white; it was so beautiful. We are just so lucky Tommy is okay. None of it even matters, except that Tommy is okay."

"If there's anything we can do," Jared offered as they stood out on the porch saying their goodbyes late that night. The burnt smell wafted through the air as they were standing out in the crisp spring night. Chickee and Jared offered him a room, if Lee didn't want to be alone. Stella was headed back to the hospital to spend the night by Tommy's bed. She had only come home long enough to take a quick shower and grab some things. Lee felt he needed to stay on the farm and tend to the remainder of the flock. Certainly, the ewes that were left were very skittish and out of sorts. Lee, Jared, and Chickee had worked together after the fire truck left to set up a fenced area closer to the farmhouse for "the girls" to stay the night. With as few words as possible, they put a lean to up, even though the forecast did not call for rain. The few sheep that were left, about forty of them, were huddled close together and baaing, their big round eyes showing their fear remained from the day's bizarre events.

Chickee couldn't wind down for the night when they got home, even though it was late. She shed her clothes in the laundry room and called for Jared to bring his in too; she wanted to get the smoky smell out of her clothes, out of her hair, out of her head. After putting the smoke-laden clothes into the washer, she went to take a shower. With her eyes, she invited Jared to join her, but he was troubled and distracted. He pulled on a clean pair of jeans and a t-shirt and said he was headed out to the workshop for a while. He couldn't sleep either.

As she let the hot water droplets fall on her head, her face, her back, Chickee closed her eyes and squeezed more tears out. In her silent thoughts, Chickee was thankful she had not arrived in time to hear the cries of the sheep as they burned to death. She felt selfish for the thought. She stood there and let the water fall down; let the steam rise up. She willed her sadness to float up to the ceiling with the steam.

The door to the bathroom opened, and Jared was there, his t-shirt and jeans shed, and he climbed in and held her close. Somehow he realized she needed his presence, to hold her on her feet, to keep her from crumpling in a heap. They held each other and let the water wash the smoke of the day away. They lathered each other's hair in shampoo and rinsed the smokiness away. They acknowledged their desire for each other, feeling secure in one another's arms, and the silky presence in this usually solitary place invited the solace they both wanted to escape into. "I don't know what I would do without you."

The next morning, after Jared had left for work, Chickee was getting ready to go in to the hospital for a linking session. The session she had missed yesterday was covered by her newest recruit, Tina. She was curious how it had gone for Tina and the young leukemia patient, Trenton. Chickee planned to look in on Tommy and Stella at the hospital. Every time she thought of Tommy, tears would well up in her eyes. She was so thankful he was going to be okay. But this was not good for linking. She needed to be able to exude positive thoughts.

Interrupting her thoughts, her phone rang. "Hello?"

"Chickee?" Although her voice was very weak and scratchy, Chickee knew it was Stella. "Are you headed to the hospital?"

"Yeah. I was thinking about having Tina cover for me again, but I wanted to check on Tommy and you."

"Well, I was wondering if you would teach me that linking thing you do. So I could help Tommy. He looks so little and broken. I just feel so helpless." Her words were broken up as she tried to talk through her tears.

"Of course, Stella. Let me confirm with Tina and be there in about thirty minutes, okay? I'll be there. Take care."

"The Walters are bringing over a casserole later. Maybe you and Jared could eat with us if you want."

"Okay. I'll see you soon. Stay strong. I know it's hard."

"Yeah, see you soon." Click.

Chickee parked, but before she left the car to walk into the hospital, she leaned back into the headrest of the driver's seat, closed her eyes, and prayed a prayer of strength for her dear friend Stella. *God, please help her make it through one day at a time. Let me help her however I can. Let Tommy heal completely.*

As she went into the building, she practiced a little self-pep talk. She knew how important it was for the patients she linked with for her mind to be clear and to exude positivity. She was trying so hard to feel positive and full of healing force today. She made the phone call to have Tina take the session with Trenton again. She tried not to be too hard on herself for not meeting her own standards under such circumstances. Instead, she thought about Stella's request. Maybe Mother's Heartbeat would be the perfect thing for her. Stella was always looking for ways to help people. This might be exactly what could help her revive after such a huge loss at the farm.

After summoning Tina's substitution for her again today, and tomorrow, and likely the rest of the week, Chickee headed toward Tommy's hospital room. Thankfully, Tina was more than willing to put in more hours working with Trenton. He was a darling little eight-year-old boy; it's no wonder their first session yesterday went extraordinarily well.

Chickee walked through the door and Stella rushed to her in a sobbing hug. "Thank you for coming. I just want to help him. Show me what I need to do."

Chickee pulled her supplies out of her shoulder bag and began teaching her best friend the skill and technique of a Linker.

A few days later, Chickee and Jared went back to the farmhouse to share dinner with Lee and Stella, and celebrate Tommy's recovery progress. As they walked toward the house, Chickee scanned the blackened skeletal heap of rubble that used to be the winter barn. She tasted the acrid tang of charred wood in the air. As she walked up the steps of the porch, she heard a little lamb baa in its tiny voice, calling to its mother. In the fenced area they had created, she saw the lamb following closely behind its mother's flanks. She recalled a detail she had read somewhere, that baby lambs recognize their mothers by smell and by *heartbeat*. A Mother's Heartbeat. *A mother's heartbeat walks around outside her body, making dangerous and risky moves without her permission.* How could Chickee ever become a mom if it was so dangerous and painful?

Chapter Five

A Surprise

2015

It couldn't be true. She refused to believe it. The little pink plus sign put her in a daze for the rest of the day. She could hardly wait till Jared got home from work. She didn't want to call him at work and tell him over the phone. This was face to face kind of news. A baby! What would he say? It seemed being older doesn't make one feel any less unprepared for a little one. Pregnant? Really? Everyone says people who are older parents make better parents, but Chickee doubted herself. She knew she was especially fond of linking with little children under one year, but how would she be with a child of her own, twenty-four/seven? How could something be so exciting and so scary at the same time!

It seemed like the day couldn't go fast enough. She looked at the clock multiple times and it seemed like only five minutes had passed since the last time she looked. Jared would be home around quarter after five. It was only two thirty now.

Chickee had to find something to occupy her time until she could talk to him. She got on the computer and looked up some information on morning sickness, diapers, and what to eat when you're expecting. She was very conscientious of what she chose for lunch. She wondered if it showed on her face. She had heard a pregnant woman had a "glow" about her. She decided to look that up too.

"This facial shine actually has a biological basis. The increased volume of blood causes the cheeks to take on an attractive blush, because of the many blood vessels barely below the skin's surface. On top of this redness, the increased secretions of the oil glands give the skin a waxy sheen," according to a Dr. Sears online.

Chickee found herself looking in a hand mirror intently, going from room to room in order to investigate her face in all different sorts of light, to see if she could see it. Indeterminate, she decided.

She decided she would call the doctor and get an appointment to confirm what she was already certain was true. Her heart felt light and excited and seemed to pitter patter unbelievably fast whenever she pondered on the mystery and amazement she was feeling.

"Hello? Yes, Chickee Lane here... Yes, Michelle Lane. Birthdate 09-23-1972. Yes....I need an appointment with Dr. McKenzie, please. I received a positive result on a pregnancy test this morning...*(!)*...Yes, Tomorrow at eight thirty a.m. That will work, thanks."

Okay, that's taken care of, she thought. Chickee wished she would have had a linking session today. It would've passed the time more quickly to have some work lined up. She tried to read a book. She couldn't concentrate on what was happening in the story, though, because her mind kept veering back to the "p" word. Pregnant. So exciting. They'd practically given up on it ever happening.

She decided to make a list of names. For some reason, Chickee seemed drawn to "R" names today. *Ronald, Rachel, Rianna, Reece, Rhett, hahaha.* Maybe she would try "M" names: *Madeleine, Matthew, Megan, Marly, Markus, Martin.*

When Jared finally got home from work, one look at Chickee's face told him something was up. "Uh oh. What is it?" he asked with a smile, because she was smiling too, and practically jumping up and down to greet him at the door and give him a hello kiss.

"Well, I have some good news. Are you ready?" She looked at him intently, and blurted it out. "We're gonna have a baby! Can you believe it?"

"Huh, are you sure? I mean, really? That's definitely news."

"Oh, Jared. You're not happy about this? I have been itching to tell you all day. I've been so excited and happy. We've always worried about having someone to take care of us in our old age, right? Are you sure you can't muster up a little happiness about this?"

"Well, it's just really big news. It's a huge lifestyle change. And expensive. Are you sure sure?"

"I have the positive pregnancy test to show you. And just in case it's a false positive, I've made a doctor appointment for tomorrow morning before my linking session. I, for one, am very happy. I wish you would be too."

"I will be. I mean, I am. It takes a little getting used to is all."

"I think you're going to make a great father!"

"Well, look at you—already doing the Mother's Heartbeat thing! You'll be an awesome mother."

"I love you."

"I love you, too."

Chapter Six

Lester

2016-2026

Reece was such a good baby. He didn't fuss; he slept through the night at only five months old. Chickee and Jared were thrilled with him from Day One. He had Jared's nose and hair, but his face was shaped like Chickee's, so when they compared baby pictures, he really looked like she did in her baby photos. His mouth was more, somehow, like his Aunt Sherry's. A small, well-formed mouth, with a distinctive valley in the center, like the perfect Gerber baby mouth of the 1980's commercials.

Of course, it was a new adventure every day. Jared had not done much diaper changing before Reece, so he was queasy at the smell of any stinky diaper. But he bravely endured the diaper stage. They rejoiced and celebrated every milestone reached, and most were reached in the 90th percentile. Reece never seemed to waste any time getting to the next stage of things. He grew up quickly, continually surprising Jared and Chickee with what he knew and what he could do.

Similar to the rest of his life, Reece was weaned early. Chickee mourned not spending more time with the tiny boy, staring at his profile as he slept in her arms. He was all too soon walking, running, climbing and investigating all sorts of things he probably shouldn't get into. Reece had big blue eyes, twinkling with mischievousness and enjoyment at every turn. He got excited over bugs crawling around on the sidewalk, and he giggled hilariously when Jared would splash the water on him at bath time.

He was fascinated with dinosaurs from very early on, and would memorize the names of all his dinosaur toys: T-Rex, triceratops, pterodactyl, brontosaurus, velociraptor, and stegosaurus. He pretended the cats were wild beasts and were chasing his dinosaurs through the trees. The cats didn't think much of this game, and wouldn't last long in tolerating the pounces of miniature plastic creatures with loud roars and romps from Reece.

When he started school, Reece could already read at a second grade level. He had a large vocabulary that impressed his teachers, but it isolated him socially because none of the other children talked as extensively as he did. None of the other kids used as big of words, so he always seemed to be talking over their heads. He would come home upset because Lindell wouldn't play with him during recess. He began to get lonely for a childhood companion. But his imagination was active enough; eventually he made up a friend for himself.

"Mom, Lester's going to stay for dinner. Could you set a place for him, please?"

"Oh? Who's Lester? Have I met him yet?"

"Mah-om. Lester is my friend you can't see, remember? He's indivisible."

"Oh, *Lester*. He's *invisible*. Yes, I suppose we could set a place for him. Does he drink milk or tea?"

"Tea, please. No sugar. He's a little overweight," he said the last part kind of quietly, as if he didn't want to offend Lester.

"Got it. Does Lester like salt and pepper on his baked potato?"

"Lester, do you like salt and pepper on your baked potato?" He said this to the empty space beside him, and waited as if he was listening to Lester's answer. "Only salt and butter. Pepper makes him sneeze."

"Okay. Dinner will be ready in just a few minutes. You two go wash your hands. And tell your father it's ready."

"Come on, Lester. Dad's in the garage working on his project. We can tell him on our way to wash our hands." He opened the door to the garage and yelled out, "Dad! Dinner's ready!" over the loud music Jared had playing whenever he worked on something in the garage.

At dinner, Jared shot curious questioning glances at Chickee when he saw the extra place setting. Reece was carefully laying a napkin in the chair next to him, as if helping Lester with his manners; he lay his own napkin in his own lap, and smoothed it out over his knee, saying, "Like this," very softly.

"Don't encourage him in that, Chickee," Jared insisted after dinner was over and Reece had gone to prepare for bed. "People are going to think he is *off.*"

"Aw, come on, Jared. You didn't have an imaginary friend when you were six years old? He's just lonesome for a playmate. He'll outgrow it."

"Yes, but, why can't he play with kids his own age? Why does he have to make up a friend instead of just *making* friends at school? What about that Lindell kid? Didn't he come over two Saturdays ago?

"Jared, Reece is more advanced than most of his peers. His classmates are busy playing house and dolls and cars, while he's ready to read his next adventure novel, or build an airplane model. Lester is someone who accepts Reece where he's at, and lets him be himself."

"Lester? That's his name for his friend?"

"Yes. Be kind. He is needing this right now. It will go away. I'm sure one of these days Lester will take a trip and 'move away.' Please be understanding of it for a while."

"Yes, *Mom.* Mom always knows best, right?"

"Right. Now go tuck him in. I'll come kiss him goodnight in a minute. Thanks, Hon."

Chapter Seven

Chickee's Family

2016

Chickee was a large woman. She always wore draping, busy printed clothes that tended to hide her size and shape. Her brunette hair draped to her shoulders with soft waves and highlights. The waviness was real, but she didn't want to admit the highlights were the artistic magic of her hairdresser. Her skin was fair, but somewhat blotched, like all her freckles from her childhood had run together to create larger freckles; at her age, these looked like age spots. Her eyes were clear and honest. A person could look Chickee in the eye and know they were getting the real story. She wasn't able to deceive, because her eyes always gave her away.

Chickee's favorite thing to wear, though, was a pair of sweats and an oversized sweatshirt that had no band at the bottom. But she refused to wear sweats in public, so she only really got completely comfortable on the weekends, and even then, only on weekends when she didn't have a kazillion things to accomplish and errands to run. Usually, she wore what she called her "teaching clothes." Nice dress pants, usually stretchy and comfortable, with a solid color shirt. Chickee believed in accessorizing. She enjoyed earrings, bracelets and necklaces, and had various costume jewelry to match almost every outfit. She really didn't have expensive jewelry. Simple, tasteful stuff that looked nice and matched her wardrobe. The few valuable pieces of jewelry she had were ones Jared had gotten for her over the years. Her wedding ring, of course, was the prize piece. It was expensive enough with its marquis ½ carat in a setting of six small diamonds surrounding it. They listed it on the house insurance as a possession of value.

Jared thought she was beautiful no matter what she wore, so she felt comfortable in not needing to impress him. It was always nice when he complimented her unexpectedly, though. He was generous with compliments, yet sincere and loving. She felt very lucky, very blessed. Even though they had met in their late thirties, they were certain their marriage was one to last through the years. They were best friends through the hard times and the good ones.

Chickee had two sisters and a brother. She grew up in sweet oblivion, not realizing some of the hard times her family had faced when she was young, but her naïveté meant she grew up an optimist. Unlike her middle sister. Karla was calloused to the world, and this hardness was something she felt was hard-earned. When she was thirteen, she was molested by one of her junior high teachers. The teacher was never formally accused. Knowing he was out there, and that there were many other sexually deviant men like him on the loose, made Karla an insecure, yet tough gun-packing thirty-something year old single gal. She wasn't sure she even wanted to get married, ever. Chickee had never understood why Karla wouldn't want to get married, though; she and Karla were often distant. Sisterhood was not a close knit bond for these two. Instead, it was like a formal friendship that was required by their parents. Once their parents had both passed on, Chickee and Karla rarely even talked to one another. In some ways, Chickee wished she could link with Karla and heal her; she seemed broken, somehow.

Eric seemed to do his own thing and was graduated and out of the house without much ceremony, but in contrast to those two siblings, Chickee and Sherry were very close. Chickee's sister, Sherry was several years older than her, but they shared a special bond that no one else in the family seemed to grasp. Sherry was very protective of her little sister when they were young. On the school bus, teenage Sherry would "mother" Chickee, defending her from all the mean little elementary boys who got great bliss out of scaring little girls with rubber snakes and spiders. Chickee soaked it up. It was like having her mom along for the ride to school. Although they attended different schools, Sherry would be there again on the bus ride home, and Sherry was always willing to ride bikes, play tea time together, or bake little rubbery cakes in the miniature oven Chickee had gotten for Christmas when she was seven.

Chickee knew she couldn't be as good at what she did with Mother's Heartbeat except for the influence of her own mother. She felt her mother would be very proud of the efforts of Mother's Heartbeat. Her mom had sometimes visited the hospital to comfort a church family who was facing a health tragedy. Although her mom rarely went into the patient's room, her presence in the waiting area of the ICU was a comfort for several families through the years. As a young girl, Chickee was never allowed into the hospital with her, but she had heard the stories as her mother came home and shared with her dad over dinner the concern and care she felt for these people.

But it wasn't only the care and sincere concern for other people Chickee had gotten from her mother. She remembered trying to cannonball off the swing set when she was about ten years old. Her brother, Eric had dared her to do it. At first, she landed it, but the momentum sent her flying forward, and she bump-bumped face first, skidding on her knees across the gravel. She ran in crying to her mother with a bleeding lip, scraped hands and knees, looking much like raw hamburger. Her mother was so gentle and soothing. She didn't scold Chickee for the foolish thing she'd done, she gently cleaned and bandaged up her knees, put some Ambesol on her swollen lip, and kissed her forehead. She told her it was going to be all right. She remembered her mother's hand on her cheek as she leaned up against her mother's chest. She remembered hearing the loving voice, and her soothing heartbeat, a mother's heartbeat.

Chapter Eight

A Change of Focus

2016

When the Mother's Heartbeat idea all began, Chickee wasn't even a mom. She had longed for motherhood many times, but it hadn't happened for her and Jared. When she was a teacher, she tried to be content with her students as her "children." This eventually backfired, though, because as time went on, the students became more interested in their iPods and Xboxes than they were in how to interact socially and maturely. She felt like if she was their mother, they wouldn't be so consumed with their electronic things. Yes, this was the 21st century and yes, they needed these skills to be successful citizens in the modern age, but she always argued nothing could, nothing would, ever replace good old-fashioned manners.

By the time parenthood was actually in their grasp and becoming a reality for Chickee and Jared, they were in their forties. For 2016, that wasn't uncommon, but they always felt awkward and *old* as parents. She knew pregnancy was supposed to be a wonder and a joy, but for her 43-year-old body, it was a burden. And when he was finally here, Reece seemed to raise himself, the independent soul that he was. Chickee and Jared seemed to stand back and watch him do his thing, and before they knew it, he was eighteen years old and ready to leave for college. Had she done right by him? Had he ever felt neglected because Mother's Heartbeat took her concentration, and left her with the headaches? Reece never seemed to resent his parents' dedication to their own lives while he was busy raising himself. He knew no other way. It suited him. So Chickee tried not to have any regrets about it.

Sometimes when she was linked with a small baby, she would try to remember back to when he was an infant. How much time did she spend nurturing him? She tried to remember a time she linked with Reece if he was sick. There was a time or two, but they were brief, non-life-threatening sicknesses, and he bounced back quickly. Reece was now facing retirement and talking about taking a boat trip around the world. That sounded like the independent boy she knew. She only wished she had linked with her own son more when he was young.

Reece always had maintained the attitude that his mother's efforts and ability as a Linker was a talent he could brag about to anyone. He never criticized it, but he didn't express interest, because he was always busy with his own pursuits. Chickee took relief in the fact he never had a problem with what she did.

She wondered sometimes, though, if he resented the time she spent nurturing *other* children instead of her own child. For this reason, she always recruited women who didn't have children of their own, or women who had lost a child and were in transition. The grieving parents' support groups were one of the best places to find women who wanted to do something positive in honor of their lost child. Mother's Heartbeat became an outlet for their unspoken love, for their overflow of parental feelings with nowhere to go.

Chickee developed a training system for all Mother's Heartbeat Linkers. This was to make sure those who got involved were really in it for the right reasons, not only for "supplemental income" or to brag on a special skill. When the hackers started taking advantage of the linking systems for the simple thrill of it, that's when the problems started.

Originally, touch was required (back in 2014) in order for linking heartbeats to occur. Eventually, Mother's Heartbeat Linkers were equipped with a wristband that could give them a "leash" to the restroom, when needed. The child wore a badge on the left side of his or her chest that the wire was hooked up to, much like the circuitry of an EKG.

Chapter Nine

Mental Illness Hurts

2092

"Here you go, Gus." Tara set his meal down in front of him, and Chickee brought her focus back to present day. *Gus. Gus. Got to remember: Gus.* Chickee forked a few carrot slices and chewed aimlessly. She took a drink of lukewarm tea and looked up over the rim of her glass at Gus. He looked at her. He smiled.

Chickee, shocked at his acknowledgement, smiled back and chewed some more. Gus pushed his mushy carrots around the plate with a spoon. He looked at Chickee again and started flirting. "Hey, we should go for a burger sometime."

She was flattered. Nobody here realized how old she actually was. She was probably old enough to be Gus's mother. Probably even old enough to have linked with him, if he had a nodule or an implant. But when you're all wrinkled and creaky-boned, apparently it doesn't seem to matter. All the years meld together. Everybody here is beyond romance anyway. It's kind of a game to preoccupy the hours. She smiled, "Yeah, with homemade fries. And a large fizzy Coke!" Chickee and Gus continued to munch down on their meal of orange through their shared daydreaming.

"And a huge hot fudge sundae for dessert!" Gus replied enthusiastically. It became more about real food than having a date, but that was okay. Daydreaming about food was always a wonderful way to pass the time.

Chickee used to be quite the cook, back in the day. She could grill some mean pork chops and fry up potatoes like nobody's business. Jared hated vegetables, so the mainstays at their house were meat and potatoes. Real mashed potatoes with lots of butter. Reece's favorite was his mom's chili on a cold blustery day. *Mmmm.* It had been ages since she had a really good bowl of chili. They never served much here with any amount of flavor or spice.

Chickee thought more on the idea of Gus actually being young enough to have been a Mother's Heartbeat child. Three years in a nursing home, and they got younger and younger! Perhaps adult linking could help a person transition into death? Chickee knew from the hacker experiences that linking with an adult was even more draining and painful afterward than any link she had ever done with a child. Could she willingly withstand the miserable migraines now, to help a few of these sickly people through their last days? The other thing she had to consider was the fact that adult linking would shorten her life. But she was already 120—about 30 years over her expected lifetime—maybe being able to *choose* this decline was exactly what she wanted.

She couldn't deny, linking again to help people would create a great sense of satisfaction that she had been missing for a long time. But Gus seemed to be fairly healthy and not suffering physically. He wouldn't be one to consider for this crazy idea she had. She knew from experience that mental frailty could not be positively affected by linking. In fact, it was only detrimental to both Linker and patient.

2021

Mother's Heartbeat grew and progressed in its first seven years. Collectively, the Linkers had helped around 800 ill children and they were constantly recruiting more Linkers to do the work. A doctor from the mental health center of mid-Missouri contacted Chickee about helping some of his younger patients.

Since it was unknown territory, Chickee asked three of her best, most reliable, successful Linkers to assist with the project. After a meeting with the board, several psychologists, and the Linkers assigned to the project, everyone was excited to see what might come of it. If they could find a reasonable, noninvasive, ethics-free way of treating mental illness, the world of psychology would change for everyone. All those techniques of positive thinking considered "hokey" by some, would in fact have research to support them if this worked.

Sharon was the first to link up with a mental health patient. Dalton was 13 years old. He was diagnosed with manic depression and schizophrenia. Sharon's instructions were to send Dalton positive thoughts and calmness of spirit as she linked with his heartbeat. When she first linked with him, things seemed to be going well. He was receptive to her heartbeat link, and seemed calmer immediately. Then something went haywire. It was as though *his* heartbeat attempted to reverse the linking, causing Sharon to have a racing heart and she suddenly started breathing shallowly and wheezing like she was asthmatic. Of course these linking sessions were videotaped for records, so when Lorna and Olivia, the two other Linkers Chickee had chosen for this project, had similar responses when linking with their mentally ill patients, caution signs went up everywhere.

Further attempts showed Linkers headaches lasted longer and the linking with mental patients seemed to give them each nightmares. That was something they had never before experienced in linking with physically ill children.

Although the mental health linking was not a successful endeavor, the Mother's Heartbeat crew did not stop trying to stretch the limits of what linking would allow. One of the big questions from the beginning was *how old is too old to link with?*

Chapter Ten

How Old Is Too Old?

2025

Chickee was the first to try linking with an eighteen-year-old, a twenty-year-old, a twenty-two-year-old, and even a twenty-five-year-old. The effectiveness of the linking seemed to diminish in correlation to the advancement of Linker side effects increasing as the patient was closer to age twenty-five. By the year 2025, they had established twenty-four was the oldest a patient could be to benefit from linking, without extreme harm and excessive side effects for the Linker.

Then there was Brenda Switzer. Her mother, Mrs. Switzer insisted Mother's Heartbeat would work for her daughter, even though Brenda was already twenty-five, almost twenty-six. She was a horse rider. Her horse came across a snake on the path and threw her off. Brenda injured her spine and doctors were skeptical of whether she would walk again.

"I *know* you can help her!" Mrs. Switzer pleaded with Chickee. "She may be twenty-five, but her heart and spirit are younger, her determination is there. Please! Just try with her. Please!"

Even though Chickee knew the headache following would be longer and more excruciating than most she'd experienced before, she had compassion for the girl, and she set up the linking sessions.

"I will try harder than anyone you've ever worked with," assured Brenda. "I know you're making a sacrifice for me, and I'm gonna show you how much it means to me by walking away when it's all said and done. Most importantly, I'm gonna ride again. Riding is my passion. I've ridden horses since I was three years old. My first horse was a miniature pony my dad got me before he died. I loved Tooth Fairy so much. Her name was Tooth Fairy." Brenda babbled on and on about horses she'd had, her friends' horses, and even the horse that threw her a few days earlier. "Talullah would never hurt me purposefully; she was just frightened out of her wits by that snake." Brenda's earnest blue eyes pleaded with Chickee to absolve Talullah the way that she had already done in her heart.

"Okay, now, Brenda, I need you to relax. Think warm, comforting thoughts of wellness and strength. I'm going to put this receptor node right here, just below your collarbone on the left. Then I'll connect with you via the wristband transmitter, okay?"

"Uh, Chickee? Is this going to hurt?"

"Oh no, honey, this is the easiest treatment a person could go through. You need to relax and clear your mind of all its busy thoughts, and make sure you focus on the heartbeat, and the healing, okay?

"Okay, Chickee. Focus. Relax. Heartbeat. Got it." She started mumbling it to herself like a mantra. "Focus. Relax. Heartbeat. Got it. Focus. Relax. Heartbeat. Got it."

After the first session of linking with Brenda, Chickee tried to hide her headache until she was out of Brenda's sight. It was almost too much. Pounding, throbbing, blinding pain, right at the base of her neck. She held back a groan and shaded her eyes as she walked to the staff sleeping room of the hospital. Once there, first thing she did was turn off all the lights except the one over the entryway. She grabbed a washcloth from the linen closet and soaked it in cold water at the sink. She let the cold water run through her fingers and splashed some up on her face. She took big gulps of water over and over again. Headaches were so thirsty. Through more groans and sluggish steps to the cot, she laid the washcloth open over her face and tried to breathe slowly. In-out. In-out. Soon the chills took over and she was shaking uncontrollably. She sidled under the blue blanket for warmth, and curled up into a fetal position with her face away from the light at the entryway. In-out. In-out.

Eventually, she relaxed enough and she snoozed for a couple of hours. When she awoke, she still felt the heartbeat pounding at the base of her neck, but it was much less powerful now, more of a dull ache. The damp washcloth was bunched up in front of her and had made a wet splotch on the cot next to the small pillow. Chickee sat up on the edge of the cot and ran her fingers through her thick brown mop of hair.

She got up, took the washcloth to the sink, and turned on the hot water. She rinsed the washcloth and refreshed it under a stream of steamy water this time. She brought it up to her face and held the warm, wet cloth over her eye sockets.

"Okay, Chickee. Time to face the world," she prodded herself aloud. Running her fingers through her hair again, this time in front of the mirror, she tried to tame it in some presentable way, and walked over to the small fridge,pulling out a bottle of water. Very early in the first days of Mother's Heartbeat, she realized she needed to drink lots of water, and avoid all sodas and sugary drinks. Rehydration was one easy way to lessen the side effects of linking.

She needed to document her session with Brenda. Surprisingly, Brenda's mother was right. Although the after-headache seemed more severe than usual, Chickee felt Brenda, despite her age, was very receptive and able to link up well. Once she finally slowed down enough and focused on the task, she was able to link with her very easily and maintain the constant "pressure" of connection. When she was able to think more clearly, Chickee decided she would look for a horse figurine to inspire Brenda in the next sessions.

"Hi, Chickee. How are you today?" Brenda's enthusiastic greeting encouraged Chickee. She had been psyching herself up all morning for the headache she would endure this afternoon. "Look at the poster my mom brought in for me. Isn't it great? That's an Appaloosa. I'm gonna have one of those someday. Right now, Talullah, she's a Paint. Very pretty, but rather common. I want to have a *rare* breed. Are you a horse rider, Chickee?"

"Well, I've ridden horses before, but it's been a very long time ago. Now, are you ready to focus today?"

"Yeah, I am. I remember: 'Focus. Relax. Heartbeat. Got it.'" She gave Chickee a 'thumbs up' sign. "Whenever you want to begin." Brenda pulled at her hospital gown until the receptor showed for Chickee to connect the wire.

"Okay, here we go. Oh, wait. I got something for you." Chickee dug through her bag for the tissue-wrapped bundle about the size of an apricot. "Here. Something to inspire you." She handed the crumpled blob to Brenda. She had looked in three different gift shops to find the right one. It was made out of blondish-brown wood, very detailed in mane and tail, and was dainty, but sturdy enough to stand up on its own.

When Brenda warily, curiously unwrapped the tissue from the gift, her mouth made a big round "Ooooh," as she pulled the beautifully carved horse up close for intricate inspection. "It's lovely. Thank you!" Chickee could tell Brenda was really pleased with the gift, and humbled at how thoughtfully it was chosen. She set it on the bedside table, then took a deep breath, and said, "Okay. Focus. Relax. Heartbeat. Let's do it."

And session two with the too-old patient began. Once again, when she detached wires from Brenda's receptor, she left as quickly as she could to avoid letting Brenda see how much pain it actually caused her. This time it took a three-hour snooze to feel human again.

Two days later, when Chickee walked into Brenda's room, she was once again met with sincere enthusiasm. "Oh, Chickee! I am so excited! I got to do physical therapy today and I worked really hard. It was almost a miracle, according to my doctor. I could stand up on my feet while supporting with my arms--we were very encouraged. I know what you're doing is helping me recover more quickly. Let's get to it!"

So without any horse talk, session three began: "Focus. Relax. Heartbeat," Brenda mumbled to herself as Chickee hooked up and put her wrist transmitter on. "Focus. Relax. Heartbeat. Focus. Relax. Heartbeat."

Chickee focused on linking. Recognizing heartbeat. Link heartbeat. The search of one heartbeat speaking to another weighed on her efforts. She thought about horses, running marathons, and walking down the street window shopping.

Healing thoughts. Heart Beat Tha Thump Tha Thump. Heart Beat Tha Thump Tha Thump. Horses running through a field of long grass. Wind blowing through your hair.

When their session was done, Brenda perceptively disconnected the wire herself. "Chickee, quick. Go rest. I know you're hurting. Thank you."

So after she'd had a long nap, a big drink of water, and a warm washcloth on her face again, Chickee looked at herself in the mirror and realized she wasn't fooling Brenda at all. But something else she realized was this: what a unique experience it was to link with someone who was mature enough to focus with her, and to express concern for the side effects *she* felt. Perhaps the older kids were more rewarding an experience than she realized.

In comparison, linking with a baby was simple, efficient, and had a much less severe after-headache. But the reciprocal pleasure of appreciation and concern was a new and unusual feeling she had only experienced in linking with an adult.

Chapter Eleven

A Comforting Friend

2026

Joan was an integral part of Chickee turning Mother's Heartbeat into a non-profit organization that could benefit many more children than it had already done in the first seven to eight years. Joan was a real go-getter. She was an accountant. She knew the ins and outs of business law and had the financial wisdom that Chickee didn't. Joan was younger than Chickee by a couple of years, but they hit it off from the beginning. They had actually met at the hairdressers, and found all sorts of things to talk about with each other while they were getting trimmed and colored and refreshed. Soon they were going out for coffee on evenings when Jared had to work late, and as time went on, Joan helped Chickee and Jared with their taxes, and helped them set up the non-profit organization for Mother's Heartbeat.

Joan was tall and thin, and had bleach blonde hair that was spikey all over. She had a very bubbly personality. She laughed loudly, cried loudly and lived life loudly. She was such a fun person to be around, Chickee knew she could call Joan when she needed a pick me up or a perk me up, or needed to be pulled out of the pity party she sometimes got into.

One day late in spring, she was looking forward to the summer, Reece was beginning his summer baseball league and Jared's company picnic was coming up. She came home after a notably difficult session with an older girl who had been the victim of a knifing on the shady side of town. Her headache seemed worse than usual, probably because of the age of the girl she linked with that day, and she was not feeling particularly chipper. She went into the kitchen, put some water in the microwave to warm for hot tea, and sat on the couch to close her eyes a minute.

She couldn't really relax though, because for some reason, Reese's cat, Mush, was yowling piteously in the back bedroom. She went to investigate what was going on with Mush. She found a drooling, wobbly, sick cat and figured she would have to take him to the vet. What could be wrong? He wobbled into the bathroom like a cheap drunk, yowling all the way. She could see on the bathroom rug where he had been sick. At first she thought he was ravenously thirsty, because he climbed up on the stool like he was going to get a drink, but then plop! He climbed in! He sat there in the toilet water and looked up at Chickee briefly with a stricken look on his face and yowled loudly again.

Chickee had had many cats in the course of her lifetime, and she recognized what was going on. She hoped neither of the other two cats had gotten close to Mush today. This was distemper. This was something that used to be controllable by vaccination, but so many people had given up on taking care of their pets properly when the economy took a sharp downturn several years ago. Apparently the virus had mutated enough, the original vaccine was no longer effective, because Mush had been vaccinated when he was younger. *Oh, Mush! Why?* Her head pounded, her eyes burned, and she tried desperately not to throw up herself as she cleaned up the catsick.

Chickee remembered from when she was little, once they were bathing willingly like this, it was only a matter of time. She wished she didn't have that memory of her childhood kitty, Goose, so sick and drenched in toilet water, wailing like a sick child. She had cried for days when Goose died. The thought of it even now, made her eyes prick with sadness, especially knowing what was in store for Mush.

She had to get out of the bathroom. She tied up the trash with the catsick and dirty rag in it, and took it out to the garage. She leaned against the car in the garage and let the auto light timer go off. Darkness. Almost silence. Only the cars intermittently driving by outside. *Oh!* How was she going to break the news to Reece when she picked him up from Little League? Chickee almost didn't want to go back in the house, because what if Mush was still yowling? She was tempted to go back and try some touch linking with Mush. Would it work on animals? Only one way to find out. She just had to ignore the raging headache from her earlier linking session. She knew she had to try it. Even though Mush was not human, he was a family member, and it would be so hard to face Reece if she didn't at least *try* to link with the animal.

She went back into the house, and at first, she didn't hear any yowling. She supposed she ought to gather up Shrek and Hito and put them in the basement, away from Mush.

"Here kitty, kitty, kitty." First two, then—*oh no*—three kitties came at the call. Mush was dripping wet and wobbling in, as if he could even eat a snack. "Oh dear, Mush." Chickee quickly scooped up the other two and set them on the stairs to the basement, and shut the door. She bent down and scrubbed Mush's soppy head, as she threw down a dishtowel to soak up the puddle he was creating on the floor. "Be right back," she told him, as if he could understand. Instead, he followed her into the entryway, where she had hung her work bag with her device and supplies.

She hadn't figured on using her linking device, but her stethoscope was in her bag, so she grabbed that and went back to the bathroom to get a towel to wrap the wet cat in. He protested briefly, but she scooped him up quickly and went to sit on the couch in the living room. She knew cats had a quicker heartbeat than children, but she didn't know what the rate should actually be, so she pulled out her PCD and voice-activated a search. "What is a normal cat heartbeat per minute?"

"A cat's normal heart rate tends to range from 140-220 beats a minute."

Chickee knew from her work that a baby's heartbeat was around 130-150 beats per minute, so she calculated that Mush's heartrate would be much faster than she was used to. But since her goal by design was to remind his body of the conditions in the womb, she technically only needed to mimic a mother cat's resting heartbeat. She decided she would run in place for a minute to raise her heartrate at least a little bit. She set Mush down in his towel, and he quickly wiggled out of it. His foamy face and watery eyes looked up at her expectantly. "Meowww!"

"Just a minute, Mush," she told him as she ran in place to raise her heartrate. "I'm trying here, buddy, just give me a sec." He paced in a circle as she ran, watching the secondhand on the clock above the mantle to tick back around to twelve. While her heartrate was still high, she scooped him up and placed her hand on his chest. He did not resist, so she spoke softly to him and told him it would be okay. Once she found his heartbeat, she held him close to her chest and exuded with all her inner force, her racing heartbeat to him. For a moment, he seemed to comply. With her eyes closed, Chickee concentrated all her effort to matching a cat mother's heartbeat for Mush. Then there was a bright burst of light behind her closed eyes. Her head felt like someone pierced a metal rod through it.

She must've fainted. When she opened her eyes, she was slumped over on the couch, Mush was lying limp in her arms. *Oh no!* She checked him for a pulse, but could not find one. She looked at the clock again. About nine minutes had passed since she sat down with him. Chickee sighed heavily and the tears pricked the sides of her eyes. *Keep it together, Chickee.* Her head was pounding and she had accomplished nothing! She had to get her mind in a better place before she picked up Reece from Little League.

She said her goodbyes. "You be good," she told him, like it was any other day. "I'll be back after a while, little guy. You just rest here." She curled him gently on the couch, as if he was just snoozing. "Bye, Baby," her voice cracked. She hoped he didn't suffer any. She gave him one last scrub under his chin like he liked best of all. Then she wiped her hands on the bath towel, and tossed it toward the hallway, so it would make it into the hamper when she got back. She stopped at the kitchen sink long enough to guzzle a tall glass of tap water before she shut the door behind her.

Of course she didn't even make it to the car door before she had tears rolling down her face. As she backed out of the garage, she felt like a failure for not helping him at all. In fact, all she'd done is progress his death more quickly. Maybe that wasn't all bad. *Sorry, Mush. I love you, but it didn't work.* Once the fever was so bad, it affected their brain anyway. She prayed a little prayer that he didn't suffer long, and that Reece would be okay when he heard the news.

She didn't really even know where she was going to drive. She didn't feel like a long drive; her head hurt too badly. She didn't feel like going to the library; she couldn't concentrate on reading right now. She decided she would see if Joan would let her hang out for a while. "Dial Joan," she told her PCD. An error message showed up. Apparently she was crying and upset enough it didn't recognize her command. She tried again, making her voice very calm and precise, "Di-al-Joan." It dialed.

"Hi, Chickee! Whatcha doin'?"

"Oh, Joan, I'm sorry. I need to hang out at your place for a little while. Are you home right now? Are you busy?"

"Oh, Chickee, what's wrong? Yeah, come on over. I'm here. I was just putting a load of laundry in."

"Okay, I'm actually almost to your street already."

"Good, see you in a sec."

"Thanks, Joan. Bye."

Chickee pulled into the driveway and composed herself. Joan would be sympathetic, but not let her wallow in the sadness. She pulled the keys from the ignition and grabbed her bag to get out of the car.

"Chickee," the good friend she was, Joan had heard the trouble in her friend's voice, and came out to the car to meet her before she could even climb out of the car. "What's wrong?"

"Oh, it's Mush. He was sick. I tried to link with him, but I think it just made things worse. I don't know how I'm going to break the news to Reece. It's so sad. He loves that cat so much. Mush loves him too. I had to say goodbye to Mush. It made me cry. Silly, huh? Crying over a cat."

"No, not silly. You are compassionate. That's why you do the work you do, my friend. Not everyone has a heart for other people's pain. Look at me: you tell me you're bleeding and I'm gonna run the other direction! I don't know how you Linkers are able to endure everyone else's suffering. It baffles me. So don't feel silly for something that is actually a gift."

"Huh. More like a curse at the moment."

"Well, how about some cookies? Cookies always make things better. I'm trying this new recipe."

"Oh, I wondered what I smelled. So you want me to be your guinea pig, huh?"

"Gee, thanks. But yeah, you can be my guinea pig. You like apples and pomegranates, right?"

"Yeah. I've never had them together, but there's a first time for everything, I suppose."

"Sure! These are made with fruit, honey, oats, brown rice flour, whole wheat flour, and sea salt."

"Sounds like a granola bar to me."

"Well, they are healthier than your average cookie. But I hope you like them. They're supposed to be negative in calories, meaning the energy you expend to digest them negates the calories involved in the cookie. Cool, huh?"

"Sure," Chickee bravely took a bite of the large lumpy disc Joan handed her. She chewed for quite a while, trying to keep from revealing on her face how she felt about it. This was a game Joan and she played. The longer she could keep Joan in suspense, the funnier it became. Joan was always so transparent and anxious to please when it came to her cooking.

"Well?" Joan couldn't wait any longer. "What do you think? I thought it wasn't quite sweet enough, but if I'm gonna call them diet cookies, then that's probably okay, right?"

"I think...." Chickee wanted to keep her in suspense a little longer. It helped to have a distraction, and she was beginning to smile a little. She knew Joan would help her get out of the funk. "I think..."

"What? Are they too grainy? What?"

"I think if I was on a diet, I would like these cookies," she smiled, knowing her answer would drive Joan to distraction.

"What does that mean? Since you're not on a diet, you don't like them? Come on, Chickee, you gotta help me get this recipe right!"

"Compared to granola bars, these are awesome," she countered.

"You don't like them, do you? Awww, I knew it. They're too blah, aren't they?"

"I wouldn't call them 'blah;' maybe just 'healthy.' Nothing wrong with that."

"Chickee, are you playing with me? Tell me, really, would you eat another one?"

"That depends: is it free?"

"Chickee! Don't torture me! Tell me the truth."

"I'd eat another one."

"Really?" Joan got excited to hear this, but momentarily wondered if her friend was still playing with her. "Really, really?"

"Yes, really, really. I think they'd be even better with more apple in them though. Dee-lish! Are you really gonna call them 'diet cookies'? I think you should come up with something more catchy. Like 'Apple Pomegranate Dessert Discs' or 'Good Choice Cookies.'"

"Hmmmm. Good Choice Cookies. You think so?"

"Sure, why not? Or wait. Maybe 'Negative Nellies,' or 'Cancelled Calorie Cookies,' or 'Granola Grands.' She was kind of having fun now. Smiling must make her head hurt less, too.

"Okay. Here, have another," Joan handed another cookie to her.

"Oh, no thanks, I couldn't. I mean, I, well..." She was playing with Joan again, but couldn't stand to see the hurt look on her friend's face any longer. "Not really, here. Let me have another. Mmmm. Yum. See? 'Negative Nellies.' Mmmmm." She actually gobbled up the second one; it tasted better than the first.

"Chickee, no more playing. Do you like them or not?"

"Yes. I like them. You're a baking genius. Thanks for sharing. And thanks for making me smile. Now I've got to go pick up Reece from Little League, then I have to go home and decide where to bury a beloved pet. But, I did promise myself, next time I have a sick animal, I will think twice before trying linking."

"Gosh, Chickee, I'm so sorry. It's not dangerous to you, is it? I'd hate to see you get hurt for wanting to help a sick pet. Or worse—not even a pet! Promise me you won't try it on a stray. Or potential roadkill. I know you! Don't do it, Chickee, please!" She supposed Joan was partly tongue-in-cheek, but partly worried she might actually extend her skills to an injured raccoon or some other wild animal. But the reaction was the desired one: she was chuckling now.

Joan hugged Chickee tightly as she got ready to leave. "Hey, you can come cry over a sick kitty anytime, okay? Just as long as you taste my experimental baking efforts!"

"Thanks, Joan. It's a deal. One sick kitty is enough, though. Let's not wish for anymore. I'll see you soon!"

"Yup. See you Thursday—you and Jared owe me dinner for that last batch of paperwork, remember?"

"Right. See you then."

Chapter Twelve

Sonia

2030

Then there was Sonia. She was the little girl with a rare skin condition called Epidermolysis Bullosa. When the slightest touch grazed her skin, it would slough off like the skin of an onion. This left her with incredibly painful, large open wounds that were oozy, and crusted over to tight, crumbly scabs when left open to the air. Poor Sonia. She couldn't be linked with through regular touch, and her skin would not withstand the sticky substance of the receptors on the wristband model. Mother's Heartbeat had to come up with something new.

This was when Dr. Newburg got involved in the Mother's Heartbeat efforts, and changed the linking experience forever. Dr. Julia Newburg was first introduced to Mother's Heartbeat when she was a medical student at Brine University Hospital. She had the idea of implanting a tiny receiver chip under the skin of a chronically ill child. That way, he or she could always link, as long as a Linker had his or her access code.

In some ways it seemed like this new development dehumanized the Mother's Heartbeat process. But one could not deny how crucial the advances were for a child such as Sonia. Since the receiver chip was so tiny, the procedure to implant was minimally invasive, and very little of her epidermis was disturbed. Then, Chickee (or another Linker) could link with her and send her the comforting and healing heartbeat she needed so desperately to overcome the constant pain and reinjury she experienced.

Chapter Thirteen

"Chickeedoo-hoo"

2092

Lots of things seemed to make Chickee cry these days. She smiled at her thoughts of Sonia, despite the tears streaming down her cheeks. Her eyes did not see Lisa in her hover chair, right in front of her, determined to get through to the television room.

"Get outta my way, you harpy!" yelled Lisa. Chickee was jerked back to present day. She didn't respond to Lisa's insult, and instead reacquainted herself with her surroundings. Sometimes she was surprised to find herself at Green Valley Nursing Facility. As she looked up at the big TV screen at the front of the large gathering room, she saw her favorite show was coming on. This was the one with the nature scenes and interesting creatures and the elevator music. *Ahh, those were the days.* Maybe the nature show was precisely what she needed to refocus her thoughts away from the past.

2030

Because Sonia experienced particularly acute pain on a regular basis, she and Chickee grew to know each other well. Chickee often felt like her post-linking headaches were especially painful after linking with Sonia, but the difference in Sonia's welfare was so obvious, she felt it was worth it. Sonia, due to her inability to move quickly or have much human contact, was surprisingly pleasant and funny to be around. She had an arsenal of jokes Chickee had taught her from her teaching days.

"Why did the chicken cross the road?"

"Why?"

"To get to the other side. Why did the gum cross the road?"

"Why?"

"It was stuck to the bottom of the chicken's foot. Hahaha. Why did the computer cross the road?"

"Why?"

"It was programmed by the chicken! Hahahahaha!" Sonia thought that one was particularly funny for some reason. "Why did the wolf cross the road?"

"I dunno. Why?"

"It was chasing the chicken. What's red and green and gooey all over?"

Chickee's facial expression changed with the change of pattern, but she smiled and played along. "I dunno. What?"

"A frog in a blender! Hahahahaha! Oh! Ouch!" In throwing her head back in a laugh, Sonia had rubbed the underside of her leg against the sheet and skin dangled off a bright red spot the size of an orange.

"Oh, Sonia, here, let me help you. You're having too much fun, silly rabbit."

"Why do you call me 'silly rabbit' all the time? I mean, why not 'silly Sonia' or 'silly willy'? That's what my Uncle Salem calls me."

"Well, back when I was your age, there was a commercial for a cereal called TRIX. The TRIX rabbit would do *anything* to get his hands on a bowl of TRIX, and he always seemed to get himself in a pinch. The kids on the commercial would tell him, 'Silly rabbit, TRIX are for kids!' He would look sheepish and give them back the bowl of cereal, then they would chow down."

"Chickee, you talk funny. 'Chow down, silly rabbit, in a pinch.'"

"Yeah, I know."

"Why are you named 'Chickee'?"

"Well, that's another story from when I was young. Sure you wanna hear this?" she asked as she put salve and a bandage over the spot on Sonia's leg.

"Yes, please! You always have strange and funny stories."

"Okay. Well, my parents named me Michelle. That's my actual name, like your name is Sonia. But when I was in fourth grade, this boy, Carl, chased me every day at recess. Grrrr. He made me so mad. Then one day the teacher changed our classroom seating to where he and I were shoulder partners. *Nooooo!* I thought to myself. But he turned out to be really nice. He wrote me a note and asked me how I spell my name. When I told him to spell it like 'Mee-chi-ell,' even though you say it 'Mee-shell,' he went to town with that and started to call me 'Mee-chi-ell' all the time. Then one day he said, 'Mee-chi-ell with a <CH> ? Ch-Chi-Chic-Chic-kee-Chickeedoo! That's what I'm going to call you: Chickeedoo!' And it stuck."

"Hahaha! Chickeedoo! I'm gonna call you that, too, 'kay, Chickee, I mean Chickeedooooo?" Sonia placed emphasis on the "doo."

"He thought it was hilarious, too. As everybody caught onto it, they eventually shortened it to 'Chickee' and I eventually accepted it wasn't going to go away. Carl was very proud of the fact he 'named' me. At our ten-year reunion, he sang a little song to me about sitting together in fourth grade with 'Mi-chi-ell, Ch-Chi-Chickeedoo-hoo-hoo!'"

"Why did Carl cross the road?" Sonia suddenly sprang one on Chickee.

"Uh-oh. Why?"

"He was chasing Chickeedoo-hoo-hoo!" Sonia sang out the answer in the same tune Chickee had shared the story, and both of them laughed out loud again.

Through conversations like these with Sonia, Chickee discovered positive linking didn't have to be a completely focused, silent or meditative effort. Sonia and she had some great times during their remote-linking sessions. Of course, she still got the headaches afterward, but she accepted them, knowing those were a part of being a Linker.

A Linker had to judge the situation when she first met a child, to see whether it needed to be a silent, meditative sort of linking, or the more interactive, jovial type, like what Chickee shared with Sonia on a regular basis for about seventeen years.

She lived longer than most children with her disease. Chickee liked to think that was a good thing. A person with her condition leads a predictably miserable life. But Sonia had regular Linkers who assisted her with pain management (and joke collection efforts).

- 47 -

Chapter Fourteen

Losing Sonia

2092

Inevitably, the sad thoughts came again. Chickee couldn't seem to keep them at bay today. She remembered the day Sonia died. It was raining. She was twenty-seven years old, and the newest treatment beyond Linkers for pain management in EB was an injection she took twice daily that seemed to give her skin more elasticity and resistance. This was important because linking was rarely successful beyond the age of twenty for the receiver. At that point it seemed to strangely have an opposite effect than healing.

2047

The innovative medical technology tangent of molecular manipulation took the controversial stem cell therapy to a molecular level of treatment. Its first success was in the treatment of multiple sclerosis. Doctors and researchers quickly realized the value of applying it to all sorts of tissue conditions. Even the annoying teenage symptom of acne was virtually wiped off the face of the teenage America with the results of molecular stem cell therapy, more commonly known as MSCT. Now that they had removed the controversy of stem cells from prenatal tissues and were able to draw it from living donors who *choose* to share it, society was much more receptive, and maybe even a little astounded, to find out all the ways stem cells could help medical technological advances.

It was raining. A twenty-seven-year-old Sonia was thankfully free to move about and live her life out loud due to the MSCT treatment. She had her own apartment, was attending college to become a medical researcher, and no longer linked with a Linker because after about age twenty, she found it helped her less and less. Of course she would never be able to play contact sports, but the difference in her life from even ten years ago was astounding. She had gotten her driver's license and bought herself a 2032 Toyota two-door sporty car. Her age belied her driving abilities. She swerved to miss a deer, veering right off the highway into a steep bank, and witnesses said that the impact practically skinned her alive. She may have only lived one or two minutes after impact. Sonia's older sister Maggie called Chickee about two hours later, and she couldn't believe what she was hearing. It just wasn't fair.

Chapter Fifteen

A New Development

2042

It was a really deep sleep, for just a nap. She had been dreaming about caramel candy. She was making lots of caramel candy and it kept getting stickier and stickier. It would stretch into foot after foot of strings of candy, and she got all tangled up in it, but she was trying to work out the knots like when her necklaces got all tangled and it would take time and patience to get them all separated out again. Then the strings became the wires of her linking device. They were so tangled and she couldn't get the knots undone. The phone rang and jolted Chickee out of her stupor. It was a dream she was glad to get out of anyway. "Hello?" (She knew who it was, because all PCDs came with caller ID standard, but she had a habit of answering the phone like it was still 1996.)

"Mom? You okay? You sound tired."

"Hi, Reece. I'm okay. I was napping. Having strange dreams. How are you? Everything alright, sweetie?" Chickee struggled to open her eyes. She rubbed a finger over her teeth; her mouth felt like someone stuffed a bunch of cotton inside and it made her words sound fuzzy. She a terrible urge to go to the bathroom.

"Yes, everything's good. I just wanted to let you know... I have a business trip scheduled to St. Louis on the thirtieth... I thought I'd stay an extra day or two and swing by for a visit. That sound cool?"

"Oh, yes. That's sounds great, Reece. It will be great to have you. Your dad will be glad to see you, too. You know he's been wanting to show you his latest contraption. This will be the perfect opportunity for you to see it."

"Uh oh. What is it? Not another shoe rack, is it? You know I have several shoe racks already, Mom."

"No, no. Nothing like that. You'll be pleased. When do you think you'll get here? I'll cook a pot of chili."

"Well, my meeting ends around 4:30 in St Louis. I'll aim to get out and beat the rush hour if I can, but if I get caught in traffic it may take me a couple hours. Chili sounds good, Mom. See you Thursday night! Love you!"

"Love you, too, sweetie. Be safe."

"I will, Mom. Bye."

"Bye, Reece." Click. "I love you," she said to no one on the other end. He always seemed like he was in a hurry. Chickee wondered if it was good for his health for him to rush, rush, rush all the time. He would be twenty-eight this year. And already he was a successful business man. She thought it was time he settled down and found a wife, but he always seemed too busy to socialize. In a way she was glad he wasn't too quick to find someone to spend his life with. She and his father hadn't met until they were in their early thirties. By then, they pretty much knew what they wanted in a spouse, and they were willing to wait to find the right person. Chickee trusted that Reece was wise enough not to jump into anything too quickly. But she was also a little concerned, because he had only had one long romance in college, and when he got burned, he kind of gave up on dating altogether.

It was a subject she couldn't really bring up to him. It tended to close the conversation window when she brought up the idea of him finding a romantic friend. Jared would be able to talk more personally with Reece. Maybe when they were out in the workshop together this weekend.

At dinner that night, Chickee mentioned Reece's visit to Jared. "Reece is going to be in St Louis and is going to stop in for a day or two at the end of the week. It'll be great to see him again."

"Yeah, I'll have to show him my newest creation," Jared replied with a smile. Chickee was excited about what Jared was developing, and he knew it. It would help her in her Mother's Heartbeat efforts. He had taken the old wrist Velcro-closure brace piece of the linking system and wired the linking tendrils into a stretchy spandex sleeve. Not only would it be more comfortable for Linkers to use, but the snug fit would insure a secure heartbeat transmission.

The idea was actually Chickee's, remembering the lunch ladies at school would wear the tight sleeves over their forearms to protect from burns. Those years of teaching continued to influence her life, and in surprising ways. The Velcro wrist brace fit only as tight as a person could cinch it up with one hand.

"It was a great idea."

"Yeah, but you were the one that made it work. I'm excited to try it out with Riely next week. It'll be ready to use by then?"

"I think so. I want to make sure the leads are functioning, and I need to check the wiring, but it's almost ready."

"Thank you. I'm so blessed to have a husband who understands these things. I can't imagine how much I'd have to pay somebody to create the idea from my descriptions."

"Oh yeah? You could pay me." Jared smiled mischievously. "A million bucks! Or a million kisses?"

"You got it!" She smooched him on the lips. "That's one. A kiss will have to do for now. I haven't made my first million dollars yet. Ha!" With a suggestive grin she continued to flirt. "Mwwaa! There's the second one. The next one thousand come tonight when you turn out the light!" Chickee beamed at him in amusement and promise as she got up to clear the dishes from the table.

Chapter Sixteen

Visiting Sherry

2042

"I'm going to go visit Sherry. She needs me," Chickee told Jared with determination. "I've arranged for Stella to take all my linking sessions this week. She graciously agreed. She's already taken over some of the management responsibilities too. Do you want to come with me? Please say yes."

"Well, let me speak with Walter. He probably won't mind. Things have really slowed down since President Chester reinstated the free trade agreement. I'll ask him this afternoon. He's getting back from St. Louis this morning."

"Okay. Well, I'm going to make two reservations for the H-Train. We'll cancel yours if he says he can't do without you for four or five days." Chickee hoped she would have time on this trip to talk Jared into retiring. She could tell his heart wasn't in it anymore. He wanted to stay at home and work in his workshop and tinker around with things. He probably didn't want to travel to Effingham with her either, but she knew he would be determined to support her through this, so he would go even though he'd rather stay home and watch TV or design some new gadget in his workshop.

Chickee got online and pulled up the website for the Hover Speed Train. It took them thirty years longer than expected, but the public transportation system finally managed to complete a quick inexpensive way to travel across most of the continent. A person could go from Seattle, Washington to Jacksonville, Florida in about 13 hours on the H-Train. The trip to see her sister in Effingham took a little over an hour from mid-Missouri at almost 230 miles per hour. You couldn't beat it for the price, about ten cents per mile. Air travel had become so expensive, it was merely for those with private jets, or the wealthy business person. As she finished up the reservation page, Chickee's curiosity got the best of her. She searched online for brain cancers and life expectancy.

Of course they don't have anything so defined as how long a person with a brain tumor will last, but she did find out some interesting information she wanted to share with Sherry. Cell phones of the 1990s to the 20-teen years were notorious for EM electromagnetic rays, and were believed to have caused many of the brain cancers people now face. Most importantly, it was now widely known that providing patients with high doses of vitamin C right before radiation therapy proved to increase the effectiveness of the radiation on the bad cells. Additionally, increased amounts of vitamin D helped the good cells to resist being ruined in radiation therapy. *Hmmm.* She would have to make sure Sherry was taking extra vitamins.

Chapter Seventeen

"And I'm Not"

2042

Chickee first realized she was not aging as quickly as others around her when Sherry, her older sister, got really sick. One would think it would have occurred to her before then. But she had always looked and acted younger than her years, so it actually caught her by surprise when one day she stood in the bathroom next to Jared in front of the vanity. She was worried about Sherry, who had to get an MRI this morning to determine how much the cancer had grown. Sherry, at 77, was having black outs and significant gaps of memory loss that were decidedly *not* due to dementia or Alzheimer's. Chickee looked at herself closely in the mirror, checking for dark circles of worry under her eyes. As she leaned in to the mirror, Jared reassured her, "You are beautiful. We took another vote. You missed it. It was unanimous. Kitties agreed: Mom wins, paws down."

As if on cue, the cat rubbed against her leg, his entire length and circled back around to rub the other side. Jared was about to retire. Retirement had not even crossed her mind. Mother's Heartbeat was thriving, and she thoroughly enjoyed her work. She had several Linkers who were reliable and effective at linking. But she could see on his face he was ready to rest, take it easy in front of the TV, maybe go on a long vacation. He had complained recently of his insides hurting. He had always had digestive troubles, but this was different, he insisted. Chickee encouraged him to go see the doctor about it, but he had yet to actually decide to do it and make the phone call. She knew him well enough by now, she knew she could not rush him on such things. He would pursue it in his own timetable. And she would frustratingly wait on him to decide it needed to be done.

As she thought about all this, she glanced several times at him in the mirror. He busied himself brushing his teeth, shaving, combing his hair, what little there was left of it. He looked like a grandpa, although Reece had yet to find a girl and settle down, so there were no grandkids yet. His thin hair was short, and mostly white. The creases around his eyes and mouth showed he had smiled a lot. His tanned face probably had a few more wrinkles than a person who had spent the majority of their work days inside, but Chickee felt like it showed what a hard worker he was. Just then, it occurred to her that he was *73 years old*. It suddenly seemed urgent to her for him to retire and enjoy life before it was too late.

Yes, they had already prepared their living wills and all the paperwork necessary for end-of-life planning. Chickee, constantly in the world of the sick and dying, was one for planning ahead. But today she felt like Jared's septuagenarian age had snuck up on them, while she had remained in her forties and vibrantly busy and youthful.

She took another look at him in the mirror. This time he caught her eyes in the reflection and a deep sense of compassion fell over his face. As if somebody turned on a faucet, they both had tears overflowing in their eyes. "I'm getting old, Chickee. And you're not."

"And I'm not," she said at exactly the same moment he said it. Her voice cracked in the saying. She felt like someone had slapped her in the face and the sting of it made her aware all in one instant that she would outlive him, long outlive him even, and disbelieving, she shook her head in bafflement, looking again at his eyes in the reflection. She covered her face with her hands as she began weeping.

He put a strong arm around her shoulders and told her everything was going to be all right. But she didn't believe him. In that instant of self-awareness, her entire world had flipped upside down and she felt all the blood rush to her head. She had to sit down. She went into the bedroom and sat on the end of the bed. Jared came and sat next to her, letting her weep, always being the strong, faithful presence he had been for her all along. Finally, she was able to talk, and she told him, "I don't want to live without you."

"Well, hon, I'm not dead yet." They both laughed a little.

"I know. But this means I *will* outlive you, doesn't it?" Hastily she sucked in air, as if an idea hit her. "Ah! Jared! You've got to start linking now. I can teach you. I mean, we've never used fathers instead of mothers, but why didn't I think of it before! Then you could stop aging too!"

"Chickee, don't you think I've been aware of this for some time? Do you really want me in my old geezer stage to stop aging here, now? There's already a gap between us. You'll tire of me as an old man, an old fuddy-duddy."

She didn't want to acknowledge he was right. He had already come to terms with this. She was the one who had to get used to the idea now. "I've got to have a conference with the girls!" Chickee realized abruptly. Why had she not seen this before? Did it take Sherry getting deathly ill for her to size up the truth of things? She shook out the feeling of surprise and tried on the shirt of longevity for the first time. A test fit. She didn't know how she liked it. And she wondered *how long* would it really add to her life? Was there a formula for the age of the person you linked with correlating to how much time you added to your life? So many questions flitted through her mind; the whole truth of it overwhelmed her.

"You know, Jared, I will never be done loving you. Don't get done here too quickly, okay? I'll never be ready for you to be gone." They held each other and savored the moment of silent understanding. *Oh God, I am so thankful for this man*, she prayed in her thoughts. *Don't take him away too quickly.*

But at that time in history, who could know he only had two and a half years left.

Chapter Eighteen

Longevity

2042

The point in time Chickee realized she would outlive everyone she loved who was around her age, and maybe even everyone who was twenty to thirty years younger than her, was the point she also realized that the people she needed to cling tightly to were her workers. Only they would be around eventually. They would be the only ones other than herself that might live long enough to support each other through all the losses of loved ones, spouses, friends, and, *oh!* Even their own children? It was such a heavy burden.

Chickee tried to avoid the thought that her life was being extended whenever she linked with a child. She worked to focus on the child's healing, the child's positive attitude; she couldn't let her own sadness at what the future had in store for her get in the way of accomplishing what she knew in her heart of hearts she was meant to do—help people. Heal people.

Stella was of course already aware of her *youngness*. She had outlived her first husband, Lee, and had remarried within three years—to somebody twelve years her junior. Her daughter had been a Linker for several years now, and neither one of them seemed to be getting older. Stella was not shocked at all when Chickee confided in her the recent revelation she had experienced.

"Well, it seemed like a gift to me. All the extending of ourselves we do in linking comes back to us in a long life." Stella kept a positive upbeat perspective on things, and that helped Chickee come to terms with what she was realizing about herself.

"But, we are going to watch all our precious ones die around us, and we'll still be around for *another* generation of deaths. It seems so ironic and unfair. Lots of people wish for a long life. Yet death after death is going to be a part of that life. It just seems so sad."

"Oh, Chickee, don't put them all in the ground before they're ready. You'll miss living your gift of long life if you're continually prematurely mourning the loss of those you love. I finally decided I was going to make the best of it and enjoy the time I have with them. Really, if you think about it, Reece could die tomorrow in a car accident. We never know what hand we're going to be dealt, we have to play the best game we can with the cards we've got."

"Yes, I know you're right. I need to quit worrying about things I have no control over."

"And worry about the things you *do* have control over, like helping a lot of sick kids along the way."

"Yes, you're right. I need to keep my head into the positives, especially for the kids we link with. Hey, Stella?"

"Yeah?"

"Thanks. I have a question for you: how would you like to take over some of the management responsibilities of Mother's Heartbeat? I need to go see my sister. Of course you could take over the management pay of things too. I'll only be paid as a Linker once you're in full swing manager mode."

"Really? I would be honored to manage the business for you. When do you plan to go see your sister?"

"Probably in about two or three weeks. Let's look at our calendars together and find out when we can do some training pieces. You already know a lot of the paperwork and scheduling stuff, but there's the governmental paperwork, the payroll, the not-for-profit disclosures, and few other things to know about." Both of them pulled out their PCDs and brought their calendars to the screen.

Chapter Nineteen

Losing Jared

2045

It hurt to watch him wither away, little by little, like sand being blown away from the desert. One day Chickee noticed his wedding ring fit loosely on his hand, and she remembered back to the time when he was so healthy and robust that it was snug on his finger. She felt like if he moved his hand a little, it might slip off. It reminded her of how he was slipping away from her, a little at a time, and far too soon.

Everyone was there, and Chickee should have been glad to see them but she was numb. After watching Jared wither away for seven months, she felt guilty for feeling pure relief when he finally passed. It was torture, seeing him suffer, knowing there was nothing she could do. When they called in hospice care, she was like a robot. Just taking care of details. Just making sure he was comfortable. And trying to talk with him when he was fairly coherent.

Thankfully, he had made all the decisions about his arrangements and funeral plans. Chickee was grateful that she didn't have to make all those decisions in her state of numbness.

Survival. That was her word of the day. *Survive today. Deal tomorrow. Survive. Breathe. Cry tomorrow. Just survive today.*

In some ways, the day reminded Chickee of Sherry. Everyone together. Everyone dressed up and so sympathetic. And her numb. It reminded her of Sherry's funeral, only two short years ago. Sherry only lasted four months after the diagnosis of her brain tumor.

Reece was the eloquent and finesse one with all the family, especially the older aunts and uncles. Chickee's family: her sister, Karla, and both her sisters' kids and their families. Eric's family, and all the cousins who had traveled from Minnesota.

Then there was Jared's family. They were all so sorry, so concerned, and tried to remain cheerful. Suddenly, Chickee was so *tired*. Like all she wanted to do was go lay down in the bed she used to share with her now dead husband and *sleep*. Maybe if she would sleep hard enough, she could sleep with him in his eternal sleep.

The hardest part was the graveside service. "Ashes to ashes. Dust to dust. Man comes from the dust, and to the dust he shall return." But when it came time to toss the handful of dirt over the box that held his body, Chickee wasn't ready for the closure. Reece tossed his handful before she could bring herself to crumble her own in her hand, and let it gently sprinkle down on his coffin, so lightly that it didn't even make a sound. It was like she didn't want to disturb him, now that he was finally free of the pain and suffering, and truly at rest.

She had wanted so badly to try to link with him when he was sick. To relieve him of some of his pain, but he absolutely forbade it. He knew it meant excruciating pain for her in an after-headache, even worse than from an ordinary linking with a sick child. He wouldn't allow her to even try.

She had called Reece to come home about three days ago. But it felt like much longer ago. Was it only the day before the day before yesterday when she and Jared had a tearful conversation and held each other before he got too ill to stay coherent? It seemed like many days had passed since that moment.

"Chickee," he said, "I love you so much."

"I love you, Jared. I hate to see you suffer this way. I wish I could take it all away from you."

"I don't. I'm nearly done here, you know. You're the best thing that ever happened to me. And I know your age, but I know you are *young* still, Chickee. You got to go on without me. Find somebody who will love you at least as good as I would, and be happy."

"But Jared, I don't wanna be without *you*. Why did things have to happen this way?"

"Chickee, find a way to be happy without me. I know you can do it eventually. Don't waste time on me. I've gotten the very best of life because I've had you. Now, you deserve to be happy beyond *us*. I'll see you again. I know it."

They lie down together, forehead to forehead as they shared these teary moments. "Oh, Jared, you rest now. I can see how tired you're getting."

Suddenly Jared was very firm and urgent with her. "First, Chickee, you have to promise me, promise you'll go on and find someone else. Be happy. Don't be lonely. Live life all the way for all the years you have. Promise me now."

"I promise, Jared," she sobbed. "I will try. I'll never stop loving you, though. You know that. I'll always love you. You're the love of my life."

"Yes, you are the love of my life, Chickee. I do love you so." There was a knock at the door. She sat up on the side of the bed, and wiped her face and tried to compose herself.

"Dad?" Reece had arrived.

"Reece. Hi, son," said Jared, his voice now weak and less adamant.

"Hi Dad."

Jared looked longingly at her before she left to let Reece and his dad talk. In their eyes passed a vow. A vow of love, and life, and...freedom.

"I'll see you soon," said Chickee. But that was the last time they talked to each other.

After Reece got to talk with his father, Jared went into a deep sleep. A sleep from which he never woke out of. The coma near the end only lasted a few hours, thankfully, and now Chickee found herself too numb to be a hostess for all the family. She escaped to her upstairs bathroom and sat on the toilet with the lid down, and wept with her face in her hands.

Chapter Twenty

Lost and Found

2047

Chickee and Jared met each other in their early thirties. They had both gotten used to being by themselves, and it was a pleasant surprise to find someone in the world that they really wanted to be with and didn't want to be without. Jared was convinced being alone and a little bit miserable was better than being with someone for the sake of not being alone. But they both knew what it felt like to be lonely.

When Jared died, Chickee took a long time to adjust to life without him. She woke up in the mornings expecting to roll over and feel his warmth. She responded with lonesome wonder at how long the toothpaste lasted and how slowly the toilet paper roll seemed to disappear. The worst part was eating. Chickee and Jared always loved to eat good food, eat out at restaurants, take friends out to restaurants, and have friends over for cookouts. After Jared died, food didn't interest Chickee anymore. She had never been a skinny person, but in only six months, she had lost almost a hundred pounds.

When Chickee went to the doctor, she cried when she got on the scale and saw those extra pounds she had always struggled with were gone. She would have rather had them all back if she could only have Jared back, too. Grocery shopping was something they always did together too. It was difficult to go down the frozen pizza aisle and not stock up on his favorites. Frozen pizzas were something she never really was fond of, but Jared could have lived on them. In fact, for a couple of years after his death, she kept a few frozen pizzas in the freezer, in hopes he might "drop by," or if he "showed up" then she would have his favorite food ready to pop in the oven.

Facebook friends were so well-meaning after Jared's death, but it got to the point Chickee didn't like to get online either. Everyone was always so sorry. Or they wanted to hook her up with someone they knew. She was alone. She had spent the first half of her life alone. She knew what it was to be alone and it was familiar, like an old blanket that's been washed and used until it's threadbare.

2092

At age 120, she had lived another life since he was even alive. Meeting in their thirties, they had always said they spent half their lives looking for each other. Chickee knew she was lucky to have the second half of his life. But who could have predicted being a Linker would mean she would have another life tacked on to that one?

2047

One day, she decided to go on Facebook and look up her old boyfriend from college. Sean tended to "stay off the grid" in the early years of Facebook, Twitter, and other online social sites. He reminded Chickee of John Conner in "The Terminator" movies, the way he stayed offline for some enigmatic reason. Avoiding having any of his information on the World Wide Web for fear of futuristic robotic organisms tracking him down in backwards time travel. Maybe not. She suspected he was trying to honor some rite of "good old fashioned livin'" without computers and technology whenever humanly possible. Which in this day and age was near to none.

On the day she looked him up, she was seventy-four. He would be seventy-three. It was a longshot. But, there he was, Sean Colburn, age 73, widowed, living in Tulsa, Oklahoma with two dogs and a small farm. She sent him a friend request.

Of course, it took him two weeks to read it and reply. But it seemed like after they had caught up on all the milestones of life:

marriage, children, grandchildren (for him), and spouse's deaths, it was like old times. He was as funny as ever. He had retired from his professorship at Oklahoma State University in 2035 and been living the "good old fashioned life" on the farm since, as she had always suspected he would. The only thing that got him onto Facebook was keeping up with his grandchildren in Battle Creek, Michigan, Seattle, Washington, and Dayton, Ohio.

Sean invited Chickee out to the farm. The idea of actually seeing him made her feel like a college girl all over again, and that was a surprising feeling. So she decided to go. It was a five-hour drive from Columbia, then another forty minutes out to his farm.

Chickee remembered him being tall and skinny, with lots of scrappy hair and a very real, genuine smile. The little chip in his front tooth made his smile uniquely his. He was surprisingly never self-conscious of it either. They always went to the Route A Diner on payday. Sean would order spaghetti with cheesy garlic bread, and Chickee would order huevos rancheros. They would sit and talk all evening long, letting the waitress refill their Coke and iced tea until closing time. They might splurge and share a dessert if there was something special to celebrate, like an A on a particularly difficult psychology exam, or his mom's birthday, even though she technically wouldn't be joining them for the celebration.

Chickee had never seen him around his mother, and back then, that had troubled her a little. It has been said a girl can look at how her guy treats his mom and she can know how he would treat her down the road if they got married. Chickee had only met Sean's dad and his sister. She always believed Sean would treat his mother wonderfully, but the other side of the token worried her too. What if he *didn't* treat his mom so great, but she had never witnessed it, and only believed the best of him because she was extremely head over heels for this guy?

Turned out it didn't matter. She ended up breaking it off when she decided not to return to college. Instead, she wanted to work and save some money. He also had some changes that drew them apart. His dad got very sick. He had to go back to the Tulsa area where his family was, in order to take care of his dad's hardware shop. He would finish his college studies in Oklahoma.

Now here he was in front of her again, same chipped-tooth smile, a little less youthfulness in his face, and a little more sorrow in his eyes. Still as handsome as she remembered, and her heart—did it actually flutter a little bit, like when she was around him in college? Or was that her old heart puttering out a little protest of all this excitement?

He showed her all around the farm. He had chickens, geese, a couple milking cows, and several goats "to keep the weeds down." He baked her a homemade pizza for dinner the first night, and the nostalgia of Jared was shading the evening. Sean's favorite food was pizza, too. Chickee was surprised at how many similarities there were between Jared and Sean that she had never identified.

Sean talked often about his wife, Clara, like she was away on a business trip and would be back in a week or two. It made Chickee wonder what her own friends thought of her, the way she dealt with Jared's death, and how she talked about him. She was glad for Sean, that he had met someone who made him happy and gave him a family. Of course he had all sorts of pictures of kids and grandkids to share. She showed him her pictures of Jared and Reece on her Facebook page, but the pictures on her PCD were mostly photos of the children she had linked with throughout the years.

Sean had written a book during his professor years. He was the lead archeologist on the dig that uncovered the ancient native American citadel of *Aldea Falinn*. (The cofounder of the sponsoring institution was an Icelander, thus the combination name was a compromise of the native and the money holder.) Sean had lots of interesting artifacts that he had collected over the years. After tending to the evening chores of the farm, they spent hours talking over all his adventures and finds. It was nearly two a.m. when Chickee looked up at the clock and realized how tired she was.

She had decided to make a "business trip" of it, and had arranged for some linking sessions at the Saint John's Mercy Children's Hospital of Tulsa. She knew she had to get some rest if she was going to be well for those appointments. They reluctantly said their goodnights and Sean showed her the guestroom on the second floor of the farmhouse. Once she had brushed her hair and teeth, washed her face and got into a nightgown, crawling under the covers was a welcome feeling. The sheets smelled like the cross between Dial soap and Earl Grey tea, and she thought they were pleasantly cool. She didn't fall asleep right away, though. There was so much information buzzing through her head from catching up all these forgotten years. Forgotten? Well, tucked away, at least. They had both tucked away each other's memory in the deepest part of the storage trunk, hidden under layers of linens and worries and fears. It took her awhile to relax and calm her mind enough to rest. She fell asleep with a smile on her heart for the first time in over a year.

Sean made a grand farm breakfast the next morning. She smelled the coffee brewing as she got dressed for the day. When she went downstairs, he had scrambled eggs, toast and homemade blackberry jam, jalapeno jelly, sausage and sliced peaches set out on the table. Of course there was fresh milk and butter as well. He had already been out to the barn and done the morning chores by the time Chickee even woke up.

"Hungry?" he asked.

"Well, I don't usually wake up really hungry. But the coffee sure does smell great. Thank you." She took the cup from him and sat at the table. Her eyebrows furrowed to the center of her brow in confusion. "Uh, I don't remember you ever drinking coffee. Have you changed your wicked ways, or what?"

"Yeah, Clara got me hooked on the real stuff—you know, fresh from beans and full of milk and sugar. Irresistible. I don't drink much of that colored water they serve in restaurants, though."

"So, what does your day hold?"

"Well, there's a fence out on the lower twenty acres that needs mending. That's the first thing. Then I've got some tools in the barn that need tending. And I've got a project going out there. I'm making something for my youngest granddaughter, May Belle. Maybe I can show it to you later?"

"Yeah, I'd like to see it. I'll be back from the hospital after about two p.m. Does that sound alright? Will you still be out mending fences then?"

"I should be back around the house after lunch. Do you have lunch plans?"

"Oh, don't worry about me for lunch. I'll be at the hospital and I'll scrounge up something there." Sean stood up with his mug of coffee and walked over to the window in front of the sink. He looked out into the distance.

"Oh. I was hoping you would be back here for a sandwich or something."

"Hmm. Sorry. Hey. How about *I* cook dinner tonight?"

"What? You don't like my cooking? I'm hurt!" he joked, and turned back around to look at Chickee with food still on her plate.

"Oh no. I just thought since you are providing all the groceries, I could at least do some of the labor. I've really enjoyed your cooking." And to prove it, she smeared a bit of jelly on the corner of her toast, and pushed a taste of egg onto her fork with it and popped them both into her mouth. "Mmm. Good stuff," she said through the bite.

"How about this: I'll cook dinner; you help me clean up the dishes."

"Wow. What a deal. Sounds great to me. I'll help cook, though, if you want."

"Well, I've gotten a little practice over the past several years. I'm happy to do it for you." Sean smiled and Chickee soaked up the sweet familiar feeling of genuine care it held.

"Okay. Thank you. I'll see you somewhere around two, then?"

"Okay. Have a great day, Chickee."

"Yeah, you, too. And thanks for everything, Sean," she smiled.

"You bet. Hey. It's really nice to see you again."

"Yeah, you too. I'm looking forward to catching up some more tonight."

As she drove to the hospital, she replayed what he said in her mind, "Hey. It's really nice to see you again." That was going to carry her through the day.

Chapter Twenty-One

A Neon Sign

2047

Chickee was going to call Sean this afternoon. Since Stella had taken over management duties of Mother's Heartbeat, she would be able to spend a few days on the coast with him. She managed to focus during her morning session with a tiny boy who had spina bifida. She spent a couple of hours in the staff sleep room recovering from the after-headache. But once she woke up and came home, she could hardly think of anything else. When she pulled up his name and hit "Call," she had butterflies in her stomach. Butterflies! At seventy-four years old! She shook her head at herself.

"Hi, Chickee."

"Hi, Sean. Guess what? I've talked with Stella. She's got everything under control here, and even sent me on a job in Galveston. So: I'm coming with you! If you still want me to come?"

"Chickee! That's great. I was hoping you would get to come. We can easily pass through Galveston for a day or two. When can you get here?"

"We don't even need to spend more than a day in Galveston. It's not a linking job. It's actually a supply trade with the Mother's Heartbeat Coordinator there at Mercy Medical Center. They are getting rid of all the Velcro strap wrist band models and upgrading to the spandex model—the one Jared developed a few months before he died." Jared was a subject she had not talked about much with Sean, and it always felt weird to say "he died." Especially considering she was about to spend several days with this man who may very well turn into a romantic interest. She felt like she was too old to have a "boyfriend," so she decided she would refer to it as a "romantic interest."

"I plan to be at your place by Thursday afternoon. Is that okay? I'll rent a car from the H-Train terminal in Tulsa, then head out to the farm."

"Okay. Let me know the specifics as you make plans regarding Galveston hospital. The only thing I have set in stone is a deep sea fishing excursion on Monday morning. You want to go with me on that?"

"Maybe." Chickee had a smile in her voice. She wasn't actually sure that would be something she would do, but she wasn't going to rule it out. Instead, she was going to take this one day at a time. That's always been good advice, so she decided she wouldn't do any different with this new, unexplored territory of a "romantic interest."

"Think about it. It'll be fun. I'm looking forward to seeing you again. See you on Thursday. Take care.

"Yes, you too. I'll see you Thursday, Sean."

She had a lot of planning and packing to do. Chickee felt a little giddy as she went to her closet and thought about what she should pack, what type of activities she would need to pack for, and how little time there was between now and Thursday morning when she would go to Columbia and board the H-Train. She decided her first plan of action was to get online and reserve a seat on the H-Train. Next she would dig out a suitcase and start packing.

She still had a linking session tomorrow morning, and she would need some recovery time, so that meant she had this evening, tomorrow evening, and early Thursday to get all her "rows in a duck." That was something Jared had always said. "Gotta get all my rows in a duck." He was usually checking to see if anybody was listening. But the reminder of him and his lighthearted humor caught her by surprise. *What am I doing? Should I be doing this? Why shouldn't I be doing this? Ohhh, if you could just give me a sign, Jared. A big gaudy lit up one that says YES or NO, please.*

She sat on the edge of the bed and gathered her thoughts together. It's been a year since he was gone. Reece already said she ought to move on and find somebody new. So Reece was okay with it. But would Jared be okay with it? They had always told each other they should "move on" if the other died first. "Be happy," she could hear his voice telling her. Interrupting her thoughts, her PCD bleeped loudly and she answered it in a cracked voice, "Hello?"

"Hi, Chickee Mom. I'm back from college! Only two more semesters and I am DONE!"

"Good for you, Bridgette! How were your finals?"

"Oh, I survived, I guess. I think they didn't hurt my GPA too badly. My eyes are tired from staring at the screen for so many hours in a row. Hey, I called 'cause I need to talk to you. Care if I come over for a while?"

"That would be great, Bridgette. I'd love to see you. Tell you what, I'll put hot tea on and we can share the last of the apple crumb cake I made on Sunday night out of pure boredom with myself. See you in a bit?"

"Yeah, I'll be over as soon as I charge the car battery. Or maybe dad will let me use his spare. See you. Bye"

"Bye, Bridgette."

Chickee always enjoyed when Bridgette came to talk. She liked how Bridgette confided in her and wanted her advice. She wondered, though, what could be on the young lady's mind that she wanted to talk right now. She figured she'd better put her favorite outfits in the suitcase now, in case she didn't have a lot of time later on to decide on what she was going to take. Then she remembered she would probably need a bathing suit. She pulled her old one out of the beach bag off the top shelf of the closet. It looked old and frumpy, she decided. And truthfully, it was probably too big for her now. But the only way to get a new one before Thursday would be to go to the store and actually try one on tonight. She would have to see. Maybe she should pack this one, and determine to look for one in Galveston or when they got to South Padre. Well, things might be extremely expensive there. Chickee wasn't one to spend more money than she had to, if she knew she could find a bargain.

She pulled out the rest of the contents of the beach bag. Two beach towels, sunscreen, citronella bracelets to ward off the bugs...and Jared's swimming trunks. Sigh. He didn't really like swimming as much as she did, but they had gotten in the hot tub from time to time at a friend's house or at a hotel. She remembered the time they had gotten a room with the large spa tub in it. Where was that? Kansas City? Indianapolis? The doorbell interrupted her daydreaming. "Coming!"

"Hi, Chickee Mom," Bridgette hugged her tightly. "I'm glad you are home. I have needed someone to bounce my ideas off of, but Mother already has so much going on, keeping in contact with the cohorts of Mother's Heartbeat and stuff, I didn't want to bother her."

"Well, I'm glad you came to visit, hon. Let's get some tea and sit down over a piece of cake. Want some ice cream with yours?"

"No thank you. I'm just going to have a bite of cake. I've had your apple crumb cake before—it's irresistible! I'm trying to eat less. But tea sounds great. I like that mango kind you had last time. Got any of that left?"

"Sure. Here we go," Chickee pulled her basket of tea selections out of the cabinet. Bridgette sat at the island on a stool and put her chin in her hands as her elbows rested on the counter.

"Okay. I wanted to ask you: well, it's about a guy..."

"I wondered if it was something like that. Tell me what's on your mind."

"Well, I've been dating Kevin for about three months now, you know." Bridgette took a sip of the hot tea when she handed her the mug.

"He's the guy you met in your Geology lab, right?" Chickee clarified for herself.

"Yeah. And I really enjoy the time I spend with him. He's such a nice guy. But just before my last final, I was in the library studying and Malcolm, from my creative writing class, stopped to talk for a while. He asked for my phone number to go for coffee sometime, and I gave it to him.

"Now I'm feeling like I'm doing wrong by Kevin. I mean, he— oh, I just dunno."

"How serious are you and Kevin?" Chickee always tried to ask more questions and limit her own advice-giving. Sometimes she was better at it than others, but she really wanted Bridgette to discover her answer on her own on this one.

"Well, we've kissed a few steamy kisses, but we mostly enjoy doing things together—studying, going for dinner, going to the movies, going for walks."

"What about Malcolm makes you want to go for coffee with him?"

"He and I were in this writing group together, you know. He has some really cool perspectives on things." As she thought about how to describe her answer to the question, her face lit up. "To be honest, he's old-fashioned. I like how he opens doors for me. He insists on carrying the heavy books for me. He has nice manners—not that Kevin doesn't—but I've had a crush on Malcolm since that writing group, and then we caught up in the library this past week. Now I find myself daydreaming about going with Malcolm for coffee, or a walk, or maybe on a road trip. In the writing class, we had to write about going on a road trip— it would be so fun to do the things we wrote about together! What should I do, Chickee Mom? I don't want to hurt Kevin..."

"Has Malcolm already called to ask you for coffee?"

"No. Am I putting "the cart before the horse" like Mom says?"

"Well, nothing wrong with thinking things through. Is Kevin someone you see yourself with for long-term?"

"We've not talked seriously about *anything*. I mean, he's great company and all, but I just dunno..."

"Now ask yourself this: Is Malcolm someone you see as long-term worthy?"

"Well, from what I know of him, yes. I want to get to know him better; I know for certain. But I feel like I'm betraying Kevin. I don't want to hurt him."

"Bridgette, I think you have to follow your heart on this one. It sounds like you and Kevin enjoy each other's company, but maybe aren't 'can't live without you' material. Beyond 'follow your heart,' I can only tell you what Jared would say: I always want you to be happy. Whatever you decide, be happy."

"Yeah, thanks, Chickee. I'm gonna talk to Kevin this afternoon. Thanks a lot."

After Bridgette's visit, she went back to the bedroom and sat on the bed amidst her packing endeavors. As she thought about the conversation with Bridgette, she realized she had her answer. "Follow your heart." This was Jared's big gaudy "YES" in neon lights; she knew it. "Whatever you decide, be happy." Chickee knew Sean well enough to know the kind person he is, and she was curious what might come of the visit. She would go, and with Jared's blessing.

Chapter Twenty-Two

Arms for Hugging

2047

At Saint John's Mercy Hospital, she arrived to find they weren't expecting her until 10 a.m. In some ways, she wished she'd known, then she could have spent a more leisurely morning with Sean. Of course, he may not have wanted to spend his morning "leisurely." He had a whole list of things to accomplish on the farm. She hoped she wasn't going to get in his way before the three-day excursion was over. She was a little afraid she was ambitious in thinking three days would be a good "reunion" stint of time to catch up. Did he really want her around? Did he enjoy his solitude as much as he seemed to? He'd said, "It's really nice to see you again." Yup. Here she was, rolling that around in her head again, as she knew she would replay it in tone and sincerity several times throughout the day.

She didn't really feel like going to the cafeteria for some so-so coffee, especially after the delicious breakfast Sean made for her, so she decided to go outside and walk the grounds of the hospital for about forty minutes before it was time to check in and find out whom she would be linking with today in the children's wing. The walk invigorated her. The weather this morning wasn't too warm or stuffy. The freshness of it prompted her to breathe in deeply as she walked and thought about all the things she and Sean had talked about the night before. The path wound around a shaded area with a bench there. An older lady sat there alone, looking out over the lawn and the flower beds. Chickee smiled at her as she walked by. The woman smiled back. "Older" to Chickee probably actually meant about her same age, but by the time she was seventy, she was already aware that she was not aging as quickly as other seventy year olds.

Chickee wondered sometimes why her years were extended. Was it something she "stole" from the young babies she had linked with over the years? Was it that she had chosen primarily youth (aged 12 and under) as her best linking focus? (With the exceptions of Sonia and Brenda.) The horrible thought that occurred to her was, what if *those children's lives* were shorter in correlation to her own being longer? Longevity gives a person lots of thinking time.

At about ten 'til ten, she took the elevator on the East Wing up to the Children's Hospital and checked in with the nurses' station there. A floor administrator whose nametag read "Rocky" was at the desk. He looked about twenty-seven, tops, and had thick, curly brown hair—all over. Chickee thought to herself two things at that moment. First, she thought the horrible middle school thought of "hairy gorilla man." She figured that must have snuck in from her teaching days back when. Second, she wondered how sanitary it might be for someone in the hospital to be allowed to be that hairy without grooming a little bit.

"Chickee Lane, with Mother's Heartbeat, here for a linking session. Do you have paperwork for me?"

"Hi, Chickee Lane. I'm Rocky." He rummaged around in several stacks to find a paper with a blue sticky note on it. After some cross-checking on another sheet of paper, he handed it to her. "Here you go. Room 4031. Down that hall and on the right. Payton is waiting for you." He pointed down the hallway to the left.

"Thank you, Rocky." She smiled. Through all that fuzz, she could see his eyes sparkled when he smiled back. A person's spirit always shines through the haze, she thought to herself. She felt a little guilty for the "hairy gorilla man" thought.

In the room, Payton, was indeed waiting for her. He was an eleven-year-old boy with one and a half arms. Chickee smiled and introduced herself. She knew right away, Payton was a person who could appreciate the "hairy gorilla man" comment. Forgetting her remorse, she thought she might have to save it for later.

"Chickee? That's a funny name. I'm Payton."

"Payton? That's a funny name, too. How are you today?"

"Well, other than losing my pitching hand two days ago, pretty good."

Chickee took that as an invitation to talk about his injury. She found if a person could talk about what happened to him or her, they were more likely to face the challenge head on and gain more healing from the sessions. It was amazing how much mental energy had to do with linking. "A pitcher, huh? Well, then. I bet you were already an ambidextrous pitcher, so this won't 'throw you for a loop,' as they say."

Payton looked at her confused and asked, "Who's they? I mean, what's am- bee- decks- trus? You talk strange."

"Yeah? I've been told that a lot. Mostly by twelve-year-old boys."

"I'm eleven," said Payton. "Well, eleven and a half. My birthday's in November."

"Oh? What day?" She made conversation while she set up the contraption she used. She preferred these earlier models still, because they seemed to get a better link than the remote versions. The remote versions always picked up a lot of interference from other electrical items around them, which made linking much more difficult. The kind of linking system with wires seemed comparatively primitive, but in Chickee's opinion, got significantly better results. "Ambidextrous means that you can pitch just as good with your right arm as you can with your left. Is that true?"

"It is now. Haha. I'm eleven and a half with an arm and a half. Whadda ya think about that?" he smiled. She was pleased to see how open he was to talking about his injury. "The doctor says I can get a prothesis after my half arm heals up completely. They make 'em computerized and everything! Probably no one will even notice, once I get to using it regular-like."

"Yeah? That's great!" Chickee preferred the earlier models of linking systems so much, she had even gotten training in repairing them. The wires would wear out, or the receptor nodes would break off and need replacing. Lorna always chided Chickee about staying in the dark ages when it came to linking technology, but she couldn't be swayed. She was convinced she did the best job with the more "ancient" models. Maybe that's because *she* was ancient, she thought to herself. Lorna, Olivia, and Sharon were all at least thirty years younger than her. They were about the age she was when she first embarked upon the idea of Mother's Heartbeat, Chickee realized. Only Stella was close in age to her, and she had been one of the first trained Linkers, so she had maintained her youngness like Chickee had.

"Is this going to hurt?" Payton asked warily, as he watched her pull all her things out of her shoulder bag and prepare to hook him up. Chickee realized she had gotten lost in her thoughts and forgotten to set her patient at ease as she got her system ready to link up.

"Oh no. In fact, it can be the best thing you've ever experienced, if your mind is in the right place. Who would've thought when they said, 'It's all in your head,' they were actually right!?"

"Huh. What do you mean?"

"Well, Payton, what do you know about linking?"

"Hmmm. Well, my doctor said it would help me heal faster if we did this at least three days in a row. He didn't say anything about using my head. Are you going to use a needle, Chickee?"

"Oh, no. Just a sticker on your chest that helps my heartbeat hook up with your heartbeat. The most pain you will feel will be three days from now when we rrrip the sticker off. You, young man, have already experienced more pain in the last two days than most people your age. I'm saying, you've reached your quota. So: no pain from this old lady, 'kay?"

Chickee put some rubbing alcohol on a long, fat, sterile swab she had removed from its packaging. "Okay, I'm going to clean your skin at the location just below your left collarbone; then I'll stick the receptor node on your chest and hook up the wires that will connect us to one another. You ready?"

"Ready, Chickee." Payton was linked up and ready to begin in no time.

"Okay, now: The first thing you need to do is focus. Focus your mind on healing and all the things a person does with arms: pitching and swimming and hugging and all the jobs a person does with two hands: carrying, catching, and typing. Focus. Next:

relax. Think of this as part of the rest your body needs to heal itself. Relax. Finally: heartbeat. Listen to my heartbeat. Allow *your* heart to listen to my heartbeat, okay? Heartbeat. Got it?"

"Okay. Focus. Relax. Heartbeat. Got it."

It always amazed Chickee how kids so easily turned her instructions into the mantra. He mumbled it again to himself, "Focus. Relax. Heartbeat. Got it."

Chickee wrapped her wristband around her forearm, making official connection with his receptor node through the wires, and let the healing begin. Focus. Relax. Heartbeat. Tha thump. Tha thump. Tha thump. Arms for pitching and writing and hugging. Hands for catching the ball and throwing it to third, typing final draft papers and handing notes to cute girls in class. Tha thump tha thump tha thump.

When their first session was done, Payton asked lots of questions, firing them off, one after the other, before she even had a chance to answer. "Are you gonna come back tomorrow?. Did you feel that? I think I could really hear your heartbeat! Do you always get good results when a person can focus as good as I did? How long will it be before they can fit me for the—new arm thingy? You think I did a good job, don't you? How does that thing work, anyway? Do you have kids? How soon will I know it's working?"

For all of Payton's ability to focus during their session, Chickee was sure he was hoarding up a bunch of energy and spewed it out one question after another in about a minute's time. "First of all, keep on thinking those positive thoughts. Second of all, I will see you again tomorrow at ten in the morning. Third, you did a great job focusing; I am very proud of you. You saved it all up, though, didn't you? I can't remember all of your questions, but the question about timing for a *pros-thee-sis* is a question for your doctor." She pronounced the word slowly and carefully so he could say it correctly.

"Pros-thee-sis?" he confirmed. "Okay. So how does this thingy work? I mean, how was it that I could hear your heartbeat? That was just wild!"

"Well, to make a long story short, our bodies are made up of all kinds of electrical signals. This linking system helps my body communicate to your body in the electrical signals it needs to help heal itself. Isn't that amazing?"

"Hmmm. I might have to look this up on the Internet. So, I'll see you tomorrow?"

"Yes. Have a great day, Payton. I'll see you tomorrow."

Chickee went right away to the staff lounge area and bought a bottled water, as her pounding head reminded her she needed to hydrate. Headaches were so thirsty. She sat in the darkest part of the lounge and closed her eyes for a little while, grateful no one was in there at the moment wanting to chit chat. She got up sooner than she normally would from a rest after a linking session, though, because she was anxious to get back to Sean's and visit some more. As she walked out of the hospital, Chickee began thinking about her afternoon and the prospect of spending more time getting reacquainted with Sean. *Arms for hugging. Hmmm.*

Chapter Twenty-Three

At Sean's Farm

2047

When Chickee got back to the farm, the screen door was shut, but the door to the house was unlatched. Her headache subsided a little on the drive into the country. She walked in and set her things down near the couch. Across the room, on the table, she saw he had left her a note. She walked over and picked it up. *Chickee—make yourself at home. I'll get back around 3 pm. There's cheese sticks in the fridge if you need a snack. Or a piece of fruit on the island. Help yourself. –Sean*

She looked at the fruit bowl and chose a mandarin orange. Vitamin C and a water would help her most. She looked in the cabinets for a glass and turned on the side faucet that hooked up to a water purifier. She guzzled the entire glass of water in one drink, surprising herself. She refilled her glass, sat at the table with the orange, and peeled it. Little bursts of sweetness popped in her mouth as she ate the bite-size sections. Every couple of bites, she took another long drink of water. By the time the mandarin orange was eaten, her second glass of water had a tiny swig left in it, and she was feeling decidedly tired. Well, they had stayed up visiting until the wee hours of the morning. She walked back over to the couch and laid down using a throw pillow to support her head. She was asleep within minutes.

It wasn't until the screen door creaked open that she awoke, a little slobber hanging out the corner of her mouth. She hoped he didn't see her wipe it away.

"Well, hello. Sorry to disturb your nap. How was your session?"

"Hi," she said sheepishly, "Sorry I zonked. Sometimes the after-headache needs a big glass of water and a nap. I had a good day. How about you? Did you get the fence mended?"

"Yeah, I've got one more thing to do up on the hill. Maybe you'd feel like walking up there with me later on?"

"Sure, that sounds nice." She looked at the clock. Three-o-five. And he didn't even wear a watch. How did he do that? "You taking a little break?"

"Yeah, about three o' clock I need a snack and a cup of coffee to perk me up for the afternoon. Want some coffee?"

"Actually, that sounds really good. Here, let me get up and help."

Without much more talk, they both went in to the kitchen counter and Sean pulled the beans out of the freezer, while Chickee got a filter out of the cabinet above the coffee maker. Soon the smell of fresh coffee wafted through the kitchen, and two mugs clinked on the counter, anxious for the hot coffee refreshment.

"Let's sit on the back porch," suggested Sean. He grabbed a couple of cheese sticks out of the drawer in the fridge and held one out to her.

"No thanks. Just coffee for me. I had a mandarin orange when I got in."

The back porch faced west. The sunlight shone brightly on that side of the house at this time of day, and the brightness reminded Chickee she still had a tinge of a headache. "I'm going to run in and get my sunglasses," she said quickly, before he noticed her cringe at the brightness. She set her coffee mug down on the little table by the door and stepped back into the house toward her purse she had set down by the couch. Soon she was back out on the porch with Sean, sunglasses neatly perched on her nose.

Their conversation continued casually for over an hour. Both of them were really pleased to get to know each other again. Sean talked about his wife Clara as if she was someone he would see again in a week or so. Chickee envied how casually he talked about her, because she still had difficulty talking about Jared without the deep longing and sadness for not being able to have him by her side. But she kept that to herself for now.

"Ever been to South Padre Island?" Sean asked her.

"No. I always wanted to go to the Gulf Coast, but well, we stayed so busy. We hardly ever got further than Branson on weekends now and then."

"I'm headed down there this June. Come with me. We'll have a blast. Well, as much of a blast as two seventy-something old geezers can have. What do you say?"

Who are you calling 'old geezer'?

"Sean, I—Wow. I'll think about it. I mean, it sounds like a wonderful idea. I have some things I have to take care of, though—with my business and all." His face showed his sincere disappointment in her answer. She responded with a disclaimer, "Hey, I'm not saying no; I just need to make sure everything with Mother's Heartbeat is managed without me. A lot of people rely on us."

"Yes, I understand. I hope you'll come. I'll make sure you have your own room and everything. I'd really like it if you came."

"Well, what about you? How do you get up and go with all the animals and the daily farm duties?"

"I have Jose to manage everything here while I'm away. He knows the place inside and out. Even the fact that Essie is rarely cooperative with the milking. He knows how to finesse her and keep her calm better than I do."

"Of course. I remember you mentioned him last night, now that you say it. Well, I guess I have a Jose. Someone who knows the business so well, they can manage it without me there. Stella has been with me since almost the beginning. She has done much of the managing side of things since my sister Sherry first got sick about six years ago. Seems like it was much longer ago. Funny how time passes so quickly, but sometimes it *feels* like it stretches out like years within years. Stella has really been a great help to me. How long has Jose been on the farm here?"

"Oh, about seventeen years now. He lives in a bungalow over the North Bend. I'm really thankful for him, too."

An extended silence between them allowed them time in their own thoughts. Chickee liked that it was not an awkward silence.

Sean looked out at the back yard, and the pasture beyond it. Then Sean talked more about Clara. He shared with Chickee how much she loved tending the flowers along the fence. "In my mind, I can see her dragging the hose out to water them. Then bending over and pulling a few stray weeds out of the soil." Chickee looked out at the color and the green and thought her own thoughts about Jared as she took another sip of coffee. It was getting cold, though, so she set it down and walked to the end of the porch. Her steps clicking on the wood brought Sean back to present day.

"So, how about we pull some dinner together, then go for a walk before it gets dark?"

She turned back to smile at Sean. "That would be nice. What's for dinner?" And they walk back inside the house to prepare the meal.

Chapter Twenty-Four

Galveston

2047

Thursday morning at the train station, Chickee worried she didn't pack something important, although she couldn't think of what it might've been she had forgotten. *Oh, quit worrying, Chickee. Go and enjoy yourself. There are stores there; if you forgot anything you can buy it when you get there.* The jitters were not for riding the H-Train. She loved to ride the speedy hover train. It was a bit of a rush. And so conveniently quick! If she drove this trip herself, she would spend over five hours on the road. On the H-Train, it took about two hours, with about three stops in between. The jitters were for seeing Sean again, and what the rest of the week might bring. She reminded herself they were old friends first, and she needed to count on that. Coming to terms with the fact that Jared would want her to move on helped her to determine for herself, she was going to thoroughly enjoy this trip. Maybe she would even go deep sea fishing!

The blare of the train whistle brought her to attention as she stowed her bags in the overhead compartment. Even though it wasn't really a whistle, but more of an electronic digital alert; Chickee continued to call it by the old fashioned name. The wheeled cart she had strapped the box of spandex wrist band devices to fit perfectly in the space between the seat and the sliding door of the train compartment she was settling into. She didn't trust to leave them in the storage closet in the train corridor. She wanted her eyes on them the entire trip. She enjoyed the ride by writing in her electronic journal she decided to keep for the trip. Her PCD was equipped with all sorts of neat things she could keep herself busy with, but she wanted to record her thoughts and emotions so she would remember every detail and enjoy it over and over again later on.

⁂

<date: Thursday, May 18, 2047>

The sky is clear, the train is fast, and I am going to be there in two hours.

She thought it sounded like she was writing a children's book. *Okay. Got to try not to critique my own writing. It's for the purpose of reflection, right?*

Sean has asked me to go deep sea fishing on Monday. I think I will go. But first, we are going to make a stop in Galveston and pick up a batch of Velcro wrist band devices. Sarah Tinker, the coordinator there, talked the hospital into funding all new spandex wrist bands, so I am delivering those and shipping the old devices back to Stella for inventory.

Anticipated best and worst?

Best: possibly kisses, hugs, even holds? I really miss affection. But not willing to compromise on "going all the way." Does he even think about those things? We may have to talk about it. Cross those bridges only when you get to them, Chickee.

Worst: wearing a bathing suit in front of him. Ugh.

⁂

The H-Train was slowing down and the electronic lady was announcing Tulsa Main Terminal. Chickee got to her feet, pulled down her suitcase from the overhead storage area, and she pulled the wheeled cart out from its little stowaway spot near the door. She was glad only one other passenger had shared this compartment with her for part of the trip. The young man spent the entire time he was seated busy on his PCD reading the paper, or surfing the Internet, or playing games; she didn't know which, but it didn't matter to her. He was polite as he left the cabin in Springfield and said, "Have a nice day." The only four words he spoke the entire trip, but that was alright with her. She didn't take it personally.

Chickee found the car rental kiosk and initiated her transaction. The ATM like device spit out a set of keys and a receipt, and she was on her way. Those jitters were making another appearance. She was only twenty or so minutes from Sean's house. She mentally made a note to herself to record this giddy feeling tonight in her journal before she went to sleep.

When she pulled up the drive to the farm, the dogs met her about a hundred yards down the lane and excitedly followed the car all the way up to the circle drive in front of the farmhouse, barking all the way.

Sean greeted her happily with an arm around her shoulders and a kiss on the cheek. "Glad you made it safely. How was your trip?"

"Blessedly uneventful," replied Chickee, as the dogs vied for her attention by alternately putting their heads under her hand for further petting, and nuzzling her leg affectionately.

"You can leave those two boxes and the collapsible cart in the trunk for now," instructed Chickee.

Sean took her bags out of the trunk of the rental car and headed up the porch steps. "Come on in. I put some coffee on, and bought a few cookies to go with it. Want a snack?"

She had a bit of a struggle getting in the door without letting the excited dogs into the house too. "What are your dogs' names again?"

"Lickle and Perro," replied Sean. "Here, let me help you. Perro! Lickle! Stay!"

"Thanks. Coffee sounds great. And I always like cookies, you know. Thanks for grabbing my bags." He set her bags at the bottom of the steps out of the way.

When they settled in with a cup of coffee and a plate of cookies at the kitchen island, Chickee asked him, "So, did you manage to break Lickle of a bad habit, or how did he get his name?"

Sean chuckled at her question. "Yes, he has his name for a habit he has finally given up a little bit. If he gets really wound up, though, he sometimes forgets his manners. I'm surprised you didn't get a slobbery bath on your way in the house! Guess he wants to make a good impression!"

They had a really pleasant afternoon. She went with Sean for a walk along the east fence line, and she fed the chickens and the dogs as he instructed, while he milked the cow and fed the goats. Later, Sean had set up some kindling and cut some wood for a backyard fire in the fire pit. They had a regular cookout with hotdogs over the fire. They roasted marshmallows and drank hot chocolate. It reminded Chickee of when they were on college group campouts back fifty years ago. Fifty years? Unbelievable! They sat under the stars and talked about everything under the moon until it got really late and the fire died down really low.

As they discussed the schedule for tomorrow before turning in for the night, she told Sean she wanted to go shopping in Galveston after they dropped off the new devices and picked up the old ones from Sarah Tinker. He, of course, said that wouldn't be a problem.

"Well, I guess it's time we hit the sack," Sean doused the fire with a hose from the backyard.

Chickee knew he didn't mean anything by it, but the comment still made her chuckle a little bit. Sean looked at her, making her giggle and titter again. He looked up into the air, thinking back to his comment. "Ah. Well. Just checking to see if you're listening!" They both laughed heartily at that and walked to the back porch, he, carrying their empty mugs and she, the leftover bag of marshmallows.

After putting dirty dishes in the sink and wiping off the kitchen counters, they said goodnight rather formally, then she went upstairs to brush her teeth and wash her face, getting ready for bed. She knew she still wanted to write in her e-journal for a while, so after mentioning the giddy feeling at the car rental place earlier that day when she was only twenty minutes from seeing him again, Chickee recorded one particular conversation they had around the fire pit in her journal that night.

<Thursday, May 18, 2047 11:49 pm>

Looking out across the yard, into the horizon, 'Do you ever talk to him like he's right there in the room with you?'

'Sometimes. Mostly when I'm crying and desperate for his input. I guess having half the conversation helps me to visualize what he might say if he was here. Do you have conversations with Clara too?' I kept my eyes facing up into the sky, watching the sparkling stars and careful not to make eye contact on such a personal subject.

'Only like you, when I'm really needing her input. I still miss her. But I try not to invoke her presence unless I'm just floundering about what to do.'

'Yeah, I know what you mean. Did you have any conversations about me coming with you this week?'

'Well, yes.'

'What did she say?'

'She said I should be happy. Whatever I do, she wants me to be happy.'

'That's what Jared said, too.' Our eyes moved from the stars and the horizon to each other. And then he reached across the space between our chairs and held my hand for a little while. But it wasn't as romantic as I'd hoped/imagined, I guess. It was more comforting. Comforting for me and for him. I like that he is not rushing me for something more, though. I think, anyway.

They got on the road rather late, so by the time they arrived in the city of Galveston, Sean was swerving in and around, trying to find the quickest route to Mercy Medical Center.

"Look at him go!" Chickee exclaimed as Sean took another yellow light through downtown Galveston toward the hospital. "I always remember you being the dare devil driver. Evil Knievel reincarnated!"

"Huh." Sean grunted in reply.

They were about half an hour behind schedule from what Chickee told Sarah as to when they would be there to exchange linking devices. Sarah had nine older model devices to trade out. Chickee brought with her six spandex models and four implant models for Galveston Mercy Hospital.

When she arrived inside the hospital, the information desk attendant paged Sarah right away to the lobby. Sarah walked purposefully up to the desk looking around for who might be the person she was looking for.

"Hi there. I'm Sarah. I'm sorry, I only have eight for you today. The ninth one is still with one of my Linkers. She has the last Velcro device and I will ship it to your main office as soon as she gets it back to the hospital here." Sarah was a bundle of energy and Chickee wanted to tell her to take a breath.

"Hi, I'm Chickee. That will be fine, Sarah. Here are your new devices: six spandex wrist bands, and four implant devices." Chickee placed a hand on the stacked boxes she had wheeled in on her collapsible luggage cart.

"Oh, yes," Sarah was excited to receive them. "We've already scheduled an implant procedure for tomorrow morning—one child with severe burns over forty percent of his body. He would not be able to wear a badge, so the implant is really the only option for him if he is to benefit from linking."

"I'm glad we could make linking possible for him. Was there anything else we can help with or troubleshoot for your Mother's Heartbeat program while I'm here?" Chickee asked.

"Well, I just found out, I do have one Linker who is trying to link with young adults on her own time. I'm not sure how we can avoid this sort of abuse, but I've got a few thoughts on it. Shall we sit and have some coffee to talk about it for a little bit?"

"Thank you, no coffee for me," (although, thought Chickee to herself, that might explain how energetic *Sarah* is!) "Let's have a seat, though. I'd like to hear your ideas."

"Yes, let's head over here. It will be more comfortable." She led Chickee over to a carpeted area of the lobby with couches and comfy chairs in really bright and variegated color patterns. They both took a seat, one in each of the chairs at a ninety-degree angle to one other, with a small side table between them. Sarah continued, "Maybe we should look into a monitor that tracks hours used—you know, date/time stamp, maybe even a GPS location stamp; something that holds every device accountable for using it the way it is supposed to be used."

"Yes, I think that's a brilliant idea," she replied, thinking for a moment about the idea Sarah had proposed. "I will take this back to the board of curators of the program, and run the idea by the engineers of our supplies, so they can get started on making the adjustments. I anticipate full support from the board. They are always aiming to make things better for Mother's Heartbeat. We'll see if we can make the next model improved with more accountability features. And if you need anything else in the meantime, give Stella a call—she will be an excellent help to you at any time."

"That sounds good. Thank you, Chickee. And thanks for picking these up. You saved me a ton in shipping fees. Why don't we head down the hall for the boxes? I've got the eight out of nine boxed up for you in my office. And I'll get the leftover one to your office as soon as Delta brings it back." Sarah quickly led the way, pulling the cart with the new linking devices down the hall, near the elevators, past the Cardiology wing, to a door on the left with "Mother's Heartbeat Sarah Tinker, Coordinator" on it. She unlocked the door and inside the small office, decorated with bright yellow sunflowers and bird houses, in one of the chairs facing the front of the desk, sat two medium-sized boxes. Sarah scooped them up and handed them to Chickee as a stack. On the top of each box, in big thick black letters, she saw the logo: 'Mother's Heartbeat' printed. "Here you go. Do you think you can find your way back to the entrance alright?"

"Yes, thank you. Best wishes, Sarah."

Sean had gone for a walk around the hospital grounds while he waited for her. The hospital had a beautiful garden trail making a half circle around two sides of the building, and it curved back around to the front entrance's edge. Chickee found him standing in the shade watching two squirrels play and romp from tree to tree. "Here, let me take those." He saw her walking toward him with the cart and bulky boxes tow.

They walked together toward the truck. Early that morning, she had expressed some concern about the truck. She was thinking they would take her rental car. She reluctantly transferred the box of new linking devices from the back of the car into the back of Sean's truck, tucking the collapsible cart in with them..

"Are you sure they'll be okay? I would be sick if something happened to them before we delivered them."

"I will strap them in tight. No need to worry about anything. Since it will be our first stop, we won't even have to be concerned about them. And the forecast for today is clear, but I'll cover them with a tarp too, if it will make you feel better."

Chickee didn't want to be a nuisance. And she didn't want to seem too overly anxious about them, so she didn't say anything else. But she did see Sean stuff the rolled up tarp down between two other snug items near the truck cab, so they would have it with them anyway.

Now, there was another dilemma. The two boxes of older model devices would not easily fit into the cab of the truck either. As Sean strapped them in the back of his truck, Chickee grew visibly concerned they should be put somewhere less conspicuous. "Aww, don't worry, Chickee, I'll strap them in tight. They'll be fine."

He drove them to the nearest Marshall's Department Store. They had seen it briefly on their mad rush to the hospital earlier. In the parking lot, Chickee took a fleeting glance back at the two boxes, tightly strapped into the back of the truck, but still so obvious and *inviting* someone to be curious about them, especially with that big black label right out in the open. She inwardly wished she would have insisted on taking the rental car instead of the truck. Even if it meant his fishing gear would've been put in the trunk too.

She tried to dismiss it from her mind and concentrate on finding a bathing suit she felt like she could wear in front of him. She told herself she was being too worrisome about it, anyway. When they got into the Women's Wear department, Sean mercifully bowed out and told Chickee he was going to look in the Men's Wear department for a couple of items, and he would meet her in the shoe aisle in about twenty minutes. That sounded good to her. Surely she could find something within that amount of time.

Actually, she enjoyed herself very much. Styles of swimwear had come full circle once again, as fashions always seem to do, and so she was extremely relieved to find that two pieces were full coverage once again. In fact, there was a decent swim tank top and shorts set of a black background and navy blue flowers in a random diagonal line. *Diagonal lines are flattering. Dark colors are flattering. This one covers more than I'd hoped to find available. There's one in my size. So be it,* Chickee thought to herself. Looking at her PCD, she realized she still had ten minutes to spare, so she found a navy wrap, a new beach towel of monotone blues, and some plastic beach thong sandals she wouldn't worry about getting wet, or even losing, since they were inexpensive. They would wash off easily from walking in the sand, too. She saw Sean a few aisles over as she finished picking out her sandals, so she waved when he looked her way.

"Find what you wanted?" he asked her. He was carrying a cotton tank tee, a long pair of swim shorts, and a pair of large mesh water shoes.

"Yes, I think so. A successful find, fortunately. Shall we go to the checkout?"

"I need to get a bottle of sunscreen, and then I'm ready, too." They walked by the sunscreen display and he picked out one without much deliberation, even though there must've been twenty or more different choices there.

After they both swiped their PCDs for their purchases, they went out to the truck. Right away, Chickee had a funny feeling about it. When she saw the yellow rope frayed and dangling off the edge of the truck, she feared the worst. She rushed over to the truck and her heart sank in her chest when she saw the top of the Mother's Heartbeat box slit open and sagging empty with the flaps blowing in the breeze.

"No! No, no, no, no. I don't believe it! I had a feeling. I—oh, I've got to call Stella. Sean. Call the police. Now."

"Chickee, I—"

"Call them. Now."

He did as she commanded without any further comment. He reported the theft to Galveston police rather perfunctorily, while Chickee talked to Stella about the records of serial numbers to report and what they needed to do next. Of course this meant she had to open the second box of devices, to see which of the serial numbers were still in her possession. And she was troubled to remember that one of Sarah's Linkers, Delta, would have one of the missing devices, but she didn't know which serial number that was. Chickee asked to borrow Sean's pocketknife while he was on hold with the police department. He insisted on helping her open the other box himself. She saw the stricken look on his face, and although they were not actually talking about it yet, she could see the apology in his eyes. She looked away, though. She was not ready to face him. How could she be so stupid? She knew better than to leave them out in plain view. She wished in hindsight she had at least had Sean put the tarp over the boxes. Then it wouldn't have been obvious what was in the box on top.

After setting down her bag of new items and her purse on the edge of the truck bed, she pulled a stray paper napkin out of her purse along with a pen, and began writing a series of numbers and letters down in a list as Stella read off from the file which devices were originally shipped to Galveston Mercy Medical Center. "Okay, thanks, Stella. I know. I know. Okay. Thanks for keeping everything going there. Yeah, I know. Okay, you too. Bye now."

Sean was on the other side of the truck bed reporting to the police officer on the phone what parking lot they were in, and that a box had items stolen out of it from the back of his truck. "Yes, the ropes were cut, the box was cut open, and four?" he confirmed verbally with Chickee across the truck, "Yes, four linking devices for Mother's Heartbeat program were taken. We are getting the serial numbers now. We need to come by there? Yes, I think we can do that. Yes, officer. Thank you. Yes, I'll do that, too. We will go straight there, then, after taking some photos here. Thank you. Goodbye."

"Well, we will need to go to the police station and file an official report of theft. I'm so sorry, Chickee. I should have listened to you..." His apology hung in the air followed by a long silence between them.

"I should have insisted we take the rental car. You could have put your fishing gear in the trunk of it, right?"

"I guess I was just too trusting. Well, we've got to take pictures here, and then we'll head over and make the report. I will pay for the loss of the devices, Chickee. I feel responsible for what happened."

"No. You don't have to pay for them. They were old and getting replaced anyway. I'm more concerned about how they might be misused. We had an incident back in 2019 where one of the Linker's sons 'borrowed' her device to 'play' with his friends. Luckily, it didn't cause any serious harm. But there are *five* devices out there somewhere now. Who knows how someone is going to stupidly try to use them to get a personal thrill. And who knows how many people might get hurt in the process. People don't understand the after-effects of linking. It's not a simple link-and-cure-it-all."

After taking several pictures of the box, the rope, the truck, and even the location, they climbed in the car and headed in the direction of the police station, according to Sean's GPS.

Chapter Twenty-Five

Reconnecting and Redefining

2047

The stolen box of Velcro wrist band devices put a shadow over her entire South Padre trip, but Chickee tried to enjoy herself for Sean's sake. The drive down to South Padre Island was tense at first, after all that had transpired in Galveston. Chickee did everything she could to remain upbeat and not let the worry bother her about the devices being stolen.

"I'm so sorry, Chickee. I feel like it's my fault. Please don't let it taint our whole weekend. If there's anything more I can do, I will do it. What can I do to make it better?" Sean pleaded with her.

"I just need to rest my worries in the fact that Stella is taking care of any details that can be addressed before I return. I need to remember that Mother's Heartbeat is in good hands. Stella told me to go enjoy myself. So: where do we begin?"

"Ice cream is a good start, don't you think?" Sean pulled over to a roadside frozen custard stand. Chickee chose the Triple Chocolate Delight, and Sean ordered a fruity concrete with mango, banana, and strawberry. They broke the tension by exchanging tastes of each other's frozen custard, and laughing at the birds fighting for the fries left on the picnic table next to theirs.

Friday evening over dinner at a water front fish place, Sean asked Chickee to tell him what happened in 2019.

"Olivia, one of our Linkers from the first era of Mother's Heartbeat, had left her linking device out in plain view at home, not thinking anything of it. Well, her son had a friend sleep over one night and after a feast of burgers, chips, soda, and home-made banana splits heaped up to the sky, they decided they were going to "play" with it. The boy who hooked up to the Linker side (Olivia's son), needless to say, had a kicker headache the next day. The other one threw up his entire evening of gorging and feasting right there in Olivia's living room. And of course that set off a chain reaction. Olivia's son vomited as well. It was not any fun for anybody, because Olivia, bless her heart, had to clean up the mess.

"It could have been so much worse. They were just innocent kids playing with something interesting. They didn't realize how dangerous it could be. Well, that early on, probably none of us did. But that incident brought about new regulations for Linkers to keep their devices in a safe place at all times. Thankfully it didn't end in tragedy the way some other incidents of misuse have.

"Since they were kids, it didn't prematurely age them, having the opposite effect on the receiver. Once a person reaches the age that it doesn't assist their body in healing, it will actually be detrimental to them. No cure there like they hoped. Just a shortened life."

Sean reserved a two-room cottage by the beach for the weekend. It was within walking distance of the shore, so after eating dinner, they walked along the beach at dusk, shoeless and enjoying the sand between their toes. Sean reached out to hold Chickee's hand as they walked, and it was a comfortable touch. Chickee was reminded about the "arms for hugging" and hoped he would want that, too.

There was a fire pit where the cottage path joined the beach, and they gathered sticks and brush to make a small fire after dark. It didn't last long, but they determined they would buy some firewood at a convenience store tomorrow and enjoy a longer fire the next night.

Whenever Chickee's mind went to worrying over what had happened in Galveston, she reminded herself that all that could be done was being taken care of, and she didn't need to let it shadow their weekend.

"What are we planning for tomorrow?" Chickee wanted to know.

"There is some fun shopping around here. And I want to stop by the marina to confirm our deep sea fishing plans for Sunday. What would you like to do?"

"I really want to spend more time at the beach. There's nothing like the sand and the waves to put me at peace. And I love to hunt for seashells. This has been a really nice afternoon. Thank you, Sean."

"No thanks needed. Thank you for coming. I'm so glad you decided to come. Do you want to have a cup of hot chocolate before saying goodnight?"

"Yeah. That sounds good." They went into the kitchen together and Sean started some water warming on the stove. Chickee pulled a couple packets out of the jar on the counter and grabbed two mugs from the cabinet. It took a bit to search for a couple spoons, and in the process, Sean found some marsh-mallows.

"Hey! Look what I found! Want one in your hot chocolate?"

"Yum! Yes, please. And we can roast the others tomorrow evening over our fire on the beach." Chickee liked that smiles came easy for them.

"Sit here next to me." Sean sat on the couch and patted the seat next to him as they enjoyed their hot chocolate. "I promise to behave myself." He put his free hand around her shoulder and pulled her closer, but kept his mug of hot chocolate in his other hand. "Remember that time we spent all day riding around looking for a fishing hole, before PCDs and GPS were a thing? I was really just content to be lost with *you*."

Chickee laughed. "Yeah, I remember that. I really didn't care whether we ever found a fishing hole either. That was a great day. But I do remember there were *too many bugs* where we stopped for our picnic. Oh man, I was so bug bit and itchy the next day!" They reminisced about many good times from the past, and soon the hot chocolate was gone.

Sean stood up and pulled Chickee up to her feet in front of him. "I guess it's time to say goodnight." He set their mugs down on the coffee table. Chickee was scared and hopeful at the same time for this moment. Sean pulled her close and looked into her eyes. "Can I kiss you?"

"I'd like that." And she did. It felt so good to have his arms around her and his kiss was warm and affectionate, just like she'd remembered. He held her close. "Mmmm, that was nice. I've wanted to feel your arms around me since we held hands on the beach this afternoon."

"I've wanted to feel my arms around you since back in Galveston when I screwed everything up. Oh darn. I wasn't going to bring it up. Sorry." He put her at arms' distance, but still had a hand on her shoulder.

"Let's not think about that. Let's just enjoy the weekend and time spent together. It's obvious we are comfortable around each other."

"Yes, I look forward to the rest of our weekend. For now, I need to get some rest. And I promised to behave myself, so I'm going to kiss you goodnight now." It was another sweet, lingering kiss, full of warmth and sincerity. Then they walked to their separate rooms, each pondering the potential romance in the air in their heads.

She washed her face and brushed her teeth out of habit, her routine in getting ready for bed. It wasn't until she was tucked under the covers and getting comfortable that Chickee thought about the fact that she didn't record any details of the day in her electronic journal. The gamut of emotions of the day were vast, and although there were a lot of imperfections compared to how she imagined it would go, there were some sweet moments, too. She noted particularly how much she missed feeling attractive to someone. She promised herself she would take time tomorrow to record Friday's events, emotions, and perspective.

She not only did this, with emphasis on including how she felt about the physical attraction between them, but she also took time Saturday night to record the fun day they had together.

<date: Saturday, May 20, 2047>

I feel giddy with happiness. It has been since before Jared was really sick that I had such a good day. We started the morning easy-going and light-hearted, not stressing about the day or how much we would fit in. After cleaning up breakfast things, I had time to sit out on the porch in the breeze and work on recording yesterday's events. We ate lunch at this little taqueria hut along the market streets. There were three shops I particularly enjoyed, especially after I decided what I was looking for: I wanted to find a great windchime to remind me of our weekend. There were so many handcrafted chimes of different styles, but I chose the most beautiful white conch and clam shell chime that has a delicate and beautiful tinkle in the breeze. It was at the first shop we went to, so we went back there at the last and picked it up, after I decided it was the one. Sean was very patient about all this. I think Jared might have been exasperated with my determination to get just the right one, and especially to go back to the first store to get it. But I think Sean maybe even enjoyed the thrill of the hunt vicariously through me. Haha.

We took time this afternoon to walk along the beach. I took a small pail that was sitting outside the cottage next to the porch, so I could collect some shells and treasures. The best thing I found was this piece of sea glass. It is about as big as the palm of my hand, rounded edges on all sides, and it is a true sea green color. Just beautiful.

I wore my new swimsuit to the beach with my wrap around my waist. It was less dreadful than I anticipated. Sean complimented how I looked, and took every opportunity to walk close to me and put his hand on the bare skin on my back, or squeeze my shoulder and smile. We even waded in the water and had a playful water fight. The waves of the ocean are mesmerizing and rhythmic. I hope we can spend some more time on the beach before we go.

We confirmed our boat for 10 am tomorrow morning. As long as the weather stays mild, we will be on the water until the early afternoon. On our way back to the cottage from our shopping spree, we stopped for groceries and firewood for this evening. Sean grilled pork steaks, potatoes, and asparagus with garlic. I made my favorite easy dessert: cheater chocolate mousse.

The fire was cozy and comfortable. The romantic breeze off the water was cool, so Sean walked back up to the cottage and got our jackets and a small blanket to put around our shoulders. We sat in the sand and roasted our marshmallows, although we actually agreed they were better in the hot chocolate than in the fire.

Overall it was a dreamy day. I didn't worry about a sick child that needed my connection, dealing with an after-headache, or even the stolen devices. Today was like an escape from my everyday life and I thoroughly enjoyed it. Sean is very complimenting and sincere. He gets this glassy look in his eyes every now and then, and I know he must be thinking about Clara. Every time Jared came to mind for me, I mentally reassured him that I was fine, I was happy, and he didn't need to worry about me. One moment though, I just really *missed* him. Even though I have such a good time with Sean, I still couldn't help missing Jared when at the second store we went to, there were several steampunk items made from old gears, metal tools, and huge nuts and bolts. It was just the creative effort Jared would have appreciated—all those things repurposed to create a fish, a crane, a coneflower.

There was one point at which I thought he wanted to talk about Clara, but he refrained. I tried to ask a question that would allow him to talk freely, but he just told me, "It doesn't matter. Let's just find another shell you like."

We had hot chocolate on the couch again tonight. It was steamier, though, not as innocent and sweet as before. He told me he wasn't going to promise to behave. But that I set the pace and we wouldn't do anything I didn't want to. I told him the problem was that maybe I wanted to, but I didn't think we should. His kisses were more urgent, demanding. Then for a moment, it was like Jared was in the back of the

room. I put the brakes on. "It's so easy to be with you, but I just have to stop." I could tell he was hurt. Sean told me he understands. But there was still a whirl of disappointment in the room. And yet, that feeling of being wanted, desired, attractive. It fills me with satisfaction in the midst of the disappointment.

Sunday was a whirlwind day, full of excitement and sunshine for both of them. Sean deemed the deep sea fishing excursion a huge success. They came away with a styro-cooler full of perch. Chickee enjoyed the thrill of reeling in two fish at once, when the sea dogs would bait two hooks on one line for you. She was surprised at the disc shape of the fish, but so thankful that the fishing guides did all the gutting and cleaning for them. Sean was all smiles with his big reel-in of the day at three pounds two ounces! They were both sunburnt and worn out when they got back to the cottage. They set aside enough fish for dinner, then put the rest in the freezer. Sean opened a bottle of wine and offered Chickee a glass. Then they each lie down in their rooms for a couple hours. Chickee thought she might take this time to write in her electronic journal, but her eyes were so heavy, once she had a hot shower to rinse off the saltiness of the sea, she just lounged out on the bed and was soon asleep.

She woke up to pans and things clanging in the kitchen. Sean was starting the prep for their fresh fish dinner. "What can I do to help?" Chickee walked in after checking her face in the mirror and brushing her hair. Sean stopped what he was doing and turned to embrace her in front of the fridge.

"You look beautiful. Want to make the coleslaw?"

"Thanks, sure. I'll get the cabbage and carrots. Onions? Red pepper?" She leaned down into the crisper to pull out vegetables as she called them off. Sean stood behind her and leaned over to pull a bottle of something off the top shelf. His purposeful closeness and suggestive body language was making her feel jittery inside. They danced around each other, squeezing by one another in the tiny galley kitchen to do their respective tasks, and Sean used every chance to place his hands on her hips as he slid by. He handed her another glass of white wine as he indicated he was taking the seasoned fish filets out to the grill.

"That was delicious. Thank you." Chickee never considered herself a good fish chef, but Sean knocked it out of the park! Between the refreshed feeling from her shower and nap, to the sexy kitchen dance while they prepped dinner, the two glasses of wine along the way, the delicious dinner spent eyeing each other across the little bistro table on the porch, then some fresh strawberries dipped in leftover chocolate mousse, the evening was another dreamy escape from reality. The breeze blew in more romantic expectation. Chickee didn't want this good feeling to end.

"Shall we take our drinks into the cottage?" Chickee was getting mosquito bit as the sun was setting. They were both full of attraction and anticipation. Soon there were wandering hands, clothing discarded; skin on skin and an urgency that both of them had thought was lost in themselves. It was hard to stop. They were both reveling in feeling desirable and the memory of bodies in wanting.

"Wait, wait, wait." Catching her breath, Chickee pulled herself back to reality. "I'm sorry, Sean." She grabbed for her blouse and pulled it back over her head. He sighed heavily, and a look of regret washed over him. "My old fashioned sensibilities demand that we only have sex within marriage."

"Marry me then." His impulsivity surprised her.

"But –how will that work? Will you move to Missouri? I'm not ready to move to Oklahoma. I don't think you are ready to give up the farm. My mind goes around and around trying to see how this can work..." Chickee realized she had mulled over a few things in her mind more than she allowed herself to believe.

"I don't know how we will work out all the details. I just know I want to be with you."

"What about Clara? At times you talk about her like she's just gone on a business trip and will be back next week. Other times it's almost like I can feel her in the room... Not just her. Jared, too. Don't you ever feel like there are *four* people in the room?"

"Yes, but one of the things I love is that I feel free to talk about her around you. And you can feel safe to talk about Jared around me. We don't have to block them out because we allow each other in."

Chickee had to think about that a minute. Wrapping her mind around what Sean said made her think maybe they could carve out a space for a unique relationship.

"It makes me sad. I'm so attracted to you, Chickee. Won't you try to think in possibilities? I remember our feeling of attachment we had so long ago."

"Oh Sean, a lot has transpired since then. We are both in very different places now. I love feeling like I'm an attractive woman again. I just put that part of me to sleep, thinking it was a thing of the past, gone with Jared."

"No, those things don't die, Chickee. If our time together hasn't shown you that, I don't know what will. We are very much alive. Why do we have to be alone?"

"Is there a middle ground? Somewhere between distant and close, friendship and passion, commitment and caution? It sounds crazy, but maybe we could find a way to be safely affectionate. Friends, but more than friends, but without fear of taking it too far, or crossing an invisible line?"

They spent the rest of the evening, late into the night, discussing lots of emotions, determining the line that passes from affection into dangerous passions, and what things are reserved only for a marriage commitment. They sat facing each other on the couch, holding hands, sincerely searching for a safe place to park their feelings for each other. The conclusion of the weekend before they kissed goodnight was that they had to avoid situations where the heat of the moment was in charge. They established some comfortable boundaries, and how to continue enjoying affection without expectations.

They walked on the beach again on Monday morning, his arm around her shoulders, and smiles on their faces. Sean and Chickee held hands on the drive back to Oklahoma.

Chapter Twenty-Six

Tracking Them Down

2047

When she returned to the office, Stella had communicated with the Galveston Police Department and given the serial numbers of the four stolen devices. By the time Chickee got back from her vacation, they had already recovered three of the stolen devices. Stella explained how apparently they had been sold on the black market in the back room of a pawn shop, as a device that would enhance the high from whatever the drug of choice was. Users were told that they could have a "two for one" kind of experience if they were connected during their high.

"Yes, but don't they realize the danger they're putting themselves into, linking adult-to-adult? Not only will they have the most excruciating migraine of their lives, but they will age themselves quickly. In a way I don't feel sorry for them if they're abusing themselves that way, but –wait. How are they linking without badges?" Chickee was upset to hear of the misuse of her invention and brainchild. *How could someone take something so important and positive and violate it like that?*

Stella answered her question about the badges. "Well, that's the kicker. They are creating a *node* on themselves by a number of crude manners and deviations from the original. One guy actually cut a slit in his skin to place the receiver end—"

"Eewww. Sanitary, eh?" Chickee, grossed out by the idea shivered in her disgust, and then shivered again at her next thought. "Are they sharing nodes that way? That could mean AIDS infection could spread through the use of a linking device? Never would I have imagined such a crazy thing, ever in my life!"

"Well, the police captain assured me the one who returned it to the police department, hoping for a monetary reward for "lost property," upon further interrogation, was anxious to get rid of it, because it kept shocking him and his partner."

"Excuse me? Really?"

"Well, apparently they wanted a 'deeper connection' and were told that linking during intercourse would enhance the experience of climax a hundred times over."

"Huh. Maybe, but only if you enjoy the pain more than the pleasure!"

"Right. So: this guy evidently had a nipple ring. He rigged the receiver end of the linking device with a roach clip, (wonder where he got ahold of one of those!) then clipped it to his nipple ring for link up."

Both gals immediately had a hearty laugh at this point of Stella's explanation. From the previous experiences in linking with mentally ill adults, both Stella and Chickee knew whatever anguish the receiver was going through, the Linker took on as their own anguish. Plus the nightmares and the killer migraines at a level never before experienced due to the link up with an adult were enough to make that a very short-lived experiment for Mother's Heartbeat.

"Guess he got more than he bargained for in that climactic moment, huh?"

"I'd say so. Hahahaha. Then there's the last story. Chickee?" Stella asked hesitantly, "I don't think they can sue us, can they, for misuse of one of the Mother's Heartbeat devices causing a *death*?"

"You're kidding me! Oh Stella, this is serious. This is what I've feared all along. We need to track down the other missing unit, and recover the one from Delta as quickly as possible. And account for all of our non-implant linking devices here, too! What happened? How did a person *die* from linking? Ohh. This is horrible. Just horrible."

"I know. I'll tell you about our inventory in a sec, but first, the girl using the third older device was actually trying to use it to heal. But she ended up *killing* her grandmother, who had Alzheimer's."

"Oh wow. We know from Rana's experience, trying to heal older people doesn't work either. Did you hear anything about a possible lawsuit?"

"Well, they told me the girl is in jail right now. But I'd say she got enough to live with—not just getting a black market device, but causing someone you thought you were going to heal with it to die instead. I'd say that's enough on a person. She may not need more than the fine for purchasing a black market item. Plus, how much did she possibly age herself by that one linking!"

"Hmmm." Chickee was thinking about the only other instance she had known of using a linking device on an elderly person. Similar to this under the table incident, the other was for the intention of healing, but no one had any idea it would result in the elderly lady's death.

Back when Mother's Heartbeat was first beginning, Rana, Chickee's first recruited Linker, had lost her baby daughter, Hannah, and wanted primarily to be paired with babies whose moms had died. Rana was a very compassionate Linker, and almost seemed addicted to linking, like she couldn't get enough of it.

But before the mental patient linking attempts, Rana's grandmother was very ill and Rana was sure a linking session with a linking device would help her.

After the linking, her grandma relaxed peacefully and passed on in her sleep that night. Rana never could forgive herself. She had been waylaid by the worst after-headache ever, of course, and didn't even find out until the next morning early when she awoke, her grandma had passed away in her sleep.

She couldn't have known that would happen. In the early days, everything was new and unknown. But Rana blamed herself, and quit linking altogether. She was afraid to link with children again, thinking she might accidentally "kill" one of them, and she knew she couldn't live with on her conscience.

Coming back from her thoughts over Rana, Chickee explained the ideas Sarah Tinker had shared with her at the beginning of her trip. Stella agreed they needed to meet with the board as soon as possible and get some cautionary guidelines set up for avoiding this type of abuse happening in the future.

Chickee could also see the direction this might take them—to where *only* implants were allowed and all the Velcro wrist band and the spandex sleeve devices were completely recalled and considered obsolete. But those were the actual preferred ways she liked to link up with patients. With them eventually discontinued, she would have to either adapt to linking remotely, or give it up. But that was a thought to deal with on another day.

Chapter Twenty-Seven

Delta Flank

2074

The phone ringing woke Chickee up from a nap late in the afternoon. She had slowed down the amount of linking she did since everything went remote in 2063. Plus, the abuse of stray unaccounted for old model devices seemed to have taken the wind out of her sails. Or maybe she was just feeling her age. Although most people would guess she was many years younger, (thanks to linking with children all those years), than she actually was—102!

As she sleepily answered her PCD, she didn't recognize the number on the display. So she answered like it was 1990. "Hello?"

"Ah, Hi. I'm looking for Michelle Lane." It was a woman's voice, although rather gravelly and weak. "My name is Delta Flank."

Delta! "This is Chickee Lane. How are you, Delta?" Now she was awake!

"Well, that's why I called. I guess you know I've had a Mother's Heartbeat wrist band for several years now..."

"Yes, I was aware of that. I wish you would've brought it back to Sarah Tinker when she requested it be returned."

"Well, you can have it back. I think it's broken, but I'm callin' to arrange to return it. I'm sorry it's taken me so long..." She broke into tears at this point and had a hard time composing herself to talk again. "I'm sorry if I hurt anybody by keepin' it. Actually," she sniffed and blew her nose. "Actually, I am tyin' up several loose ends lately. I need some closure because I'm.... I'm...dyin'." She wept loudly now and Chickee was silent as she waited for Delta to continue. "My doctor says my body is like a ninety-year-old lady, even though I'm only fifty-something."

"Delta, were you using the device to link with other adults?"

"Yes—I know it was wrong, but I was so addicted to the drugs, I didn't care."

"Well, all our experience at Mother's Heartbeat shows linking with adults is detrimental to a Linker's health, as well as the person you link with. It not only gives you the most awful after-headache, it also prematurely ages you. Linking with adults seems to be able to negate all the years you may have added by linking to assist children in their healing. How long did you link with children as a Mother's Heartbeat Linker?"

Delta held back a sob and seemed to sniff and hiccup, then answered piteously, "I know it's all my fault. I just want to get this unit to its rightful owner. I only linked with thirty or so children in the year I was with Mother's Heartbeat, so I know I gone and ruined it for myself. Just tell me: how do I get this back to you?" Delta's demeanor changed abruptly to anger at this point.

Chickee knew Delta was angry at herself though, so she didn't take it personally. Truthfully, she didn't have much sympathy for Delta either, though. "Delta, where are you now? I probably need you to write the address down to ship the device to, as soon as you can. Where do you live now?"

"I'm in St Louis now. I had to get out of Texas, away from my life there. Had to make a new start." She seemed to have calmed down by Chickee's patient and soft voice with her.

"Okay, here's another option: Why don't we meet in Wentsville? There's a little Italian Restaurant with a large parking lot off the main freeway exit. I'll pick up the device from you there. When could you meet me?"

"Um, I could have my grandson drive me there on Wednesday. Can we meet early? Like nine in the mornin'? Mornin's are better for me."

Chickee thought she might have Stella's daughter Bridgette or one of the other Linkers drive her, whoever wasn't linking on Wednesday morning. "Yes, I'll meet you there at nine. Hey, Delta, can I ask you to do one more thing? For me?"

"Okay....what is it?"

"I want to hear about your experiences. Every linking experience helps us understand more about what we have and what we do and what we can do. Will you do that for me? No judgments made. But I need the info."

"I dunno....I'll think about it."

"Please do. It could help the entire Mother's Heartbeat community including future patients and Linkers, for us to know every possible scenario."

"So—Wednesday at nine, right?"

"Right. Italian Restaurant parking lot—on the Wentsville Parkway exit. See you there, Delta."

Chickee called Bridgette and asked who was on the schedule for linking on Wednesday, and told her about how she would need a driver to Wentsville. Bridgette said her daughter, Ellie, had gotten her driver's license last week, and would jump at the opportunity to drive long distance. She arranged for Ellie to pick her up at 7 am, and they would head East on Wednesday morning.

Once it was arranged, Chickee got some dinner for herself and sat down to eat. She got to thinking about what she knew about Delta. Back in 2046, she was twentyish, so now she would be right around fifty-two, fifty-three. She wondered what type of premature aging symptoms Delta had, what she would look like, and how much would she be willing to share on Wednesday about all of what had gone on with her.

Chickee enjoyed the visit with Ellie on the early drive to Wentzville on Wednesday morning. They arrived about twenty minutes early, so they went through the drive-thru at McDonald's and got two coffees, and a hot chocolate for Ellie.

Ellie turned off the engine in Romano's Lasagne Kitchen parking lot, and another vehicle pulled up. It was the old-fashioned gasoline and rubber tires type, so it had to be a late 1990s model, some sort of SUV. They must've had a bumpy ride to get here, thought Chickee, because asphalt roads were rarely maintained anymore, since the development of hover technology.

She had driven a vehicle much like it for several years, back in the days when she was a teacher, before Mother's Heartbeat.

The front passenger door creaked open and a middle-aged man got out. He opened the passenger door behind his and offered a hand to Delta as she slowly stepped out of the car.

To Chickee, the lady looked as old as she herself was in birthdays! Her skin was very loose on her frame, and very dark, dry and wrinkled. It seemed as though perhaps she had at one time weighed much more than what her tiny frame held now. She somewhat resembled those Shar Pei dogs that had rolls and rolls of skin. Her eyes looked dark and cloudy. Tired eyes, thought Chickee. She was wearing an old fashioned blue women's pantsuit that fit her quite well, actually. It looked made of scratchy polyester fabric, though, like from the 1970s. She had only one piece of jewelry on. It was a mother's necklace with three stones set in tiny silver shoes dangling from a silver chain necklace.

In contrast to her dark skin, Delta's white white hair was startling to Chickee. It was like they didn't fit together on the same person.

She got out of Ellie's vehicle and stood in front of it, in plain view to greet Delta as she walked slowly around to the front of the old SUV. Chickee saw she was holding a KROGER's bag over her wrist.

"Hello, Delta."

"Hello. Chickee?"

"Yes, it's me. Is that the device?"

"Yes, here you go. Long overdue." She handed the bag to Chickee.

"Thank you. I got an extra coffee at McDonald's a moment ago. It's still hot. Would you have a cup of coffee with me?"

"Yes, thank you. I'll take coffee. Wanna sit in the truck then?"

"Sure, that's fine. Do you take sugar or creamer? I got a couple packs, just in case." Chickee took the KROGER's bag to Ellie's vehicle, dropped it into the backseat, and brought the coffee back out with her.

"Yes, please. Both, thank you. I'll have the kids stand out while we sit in the backseat. How 'bout that?"

"Yes, that'll be fine." Indeed, Chickee realized there were three other people in the SUV besides Delta. She had only seen the two in the front and Delta earlier when they drove up.

Once they got settled into the backseat as best they could, and Delta had doctored up her coffee with the remaining sugar and creamer packets, Delta got to the point rather surprisingly fast. "So, I guess you wanna hear 'bout linkin' with an adult, huh?"

She took Chickee aback by being so blunt and to the point. She thought she would have to drag it out of Delta.

"Well, I guess I better start at the beginnin'. My son was only nineteen when I first started with Mother's Heartbeat. He actually borrowed the device without my knowledge when I was home sick with the flu one week. I wasn't using it consistently because I was sick, so I wasn't aware it was gone until I needed it to go back to the hospital the followin' Tuesday. At that time, I's jus' figurin' maybe I'd left it at the hospital in my staff locker. But several days go by and I can't track it down. Sarah dismissed me after I missed three linkin' sessions due to not havin' my device with me."

"Only about a month later, when I was workin' at the Golden Hills Nursing Home, did Torrone admit to me that he had it and he had 'altered' it for his own use. I told him at that time I didn't want nothing to do with it. He was on his own and I didn't wanna see it again.

"I saw him getting' weaker and weaker over time, goin' downhill, but I thought it was all the drugs he was into. I told him I wash my hands of the whole deal. He was angry of course. Told me he never be back if his momma didn't care enough to help him out. I told him I wasn't gonna be a part of his self-destroyin' ways.

"Torrone left and I didn't see him for several years after that. Then one day this middle aged man shows up on my doorstep and I recognize somethin' in his eyes. Torrone!

'Momma!' he said, 'I need your help.' He was so bottom o' the bucket, I had to do somethin'. So I made him promise to get into drug rehab and I'd try to help him. By this time, he was twenty-seven, but he lookin' forty-eight or fifty in his face.

After his thirty days in rehab, he came back home. He gave me the device and said now it was my turn. I knew from my Mother's Heartbeat trainin' that linkin' with someone over twenty years old could be a dangerous thing. But I had to help my boy.

That first linking session was painful. He swore it helped him. So even though I had a horrible after headache—the worst ever—I did it several more times. Then one time he try to hide he be high. When I link with him that time, I felt his high. I liked it. I din' feel no after-headache. It was so much better than the pain.

Pretty soon, against what I know be right, we were linkin' whenever he was high. I told myself it was okay because I wasn't really puttin' drugs into my body. I was so out of sorts afterward, the after-headaches weren't as bad—I just slept 'em off. I din' even care no more. My own boy was usin' drugs, and I was usin' him to get my own high. He was payin' in his health. But I din' realize I was payin' in mine, too. The youngness I had from linkin' to those babies that year was all reversed and worse.

A year ago, I look in the mirror and I tell myself, 'Delta, you gotta make some changes, girl. Delta, you needa straighten out the wrong you done.'

So I been lookin' for you, to give the device back. I can't get back my youth, and Torrone, well, you saw him. He's clean now. Me too. But we both so feeble and *old.* When a person get old, they wanna right the wrongs they done. And that's what I'm tryin' to do."

Chickee realized in her inner astonishment, Delta *needed* to talk, like she was at confession for a Catholic. She needed absolution from what she'd done.

"Did the device get used at other times, too, during the last thirty years?" Chickee asked her.

"Well, there was that one time. My grandson, Jerome, was so sick with the avian flu—remember that epidemic in 2057? I linked with him several times to pull him through the worst of it. That might actually be what has kept me alive this long. He was only seven when I linked with him then."

"It's good to hear it was used for some good as well, over the years. That's what it was designed for, after all. You mentioned some 'alterations'? What did Torrone do to alter it for his personal use? And how did you get it to work for helping Jerome?"

"Well, back when I got the device, the only link up was by badge. Torrone taped an old badge to a piece of metal on a belt, then belted it around his chest for effective linkage. Cinched tight, you know? I guess one of his friends would wear the wrist band while he wore the belt. Eventually we duct taped them together, and added a piece of metal on the inside of the belt to be a better conductor.

"When Jerome was so sick, I ripped all that stuff off, and did the meter test on it, like we were taught in the basic maintenance trainin'. It seemed to work alright. I had a different nursing aide job by then, so I managed to get my hands on some EKG badges on the low down, if you know what I mean. So at least I was able to help my Jerome with it."

"Yes, at least there's that. Anything else I should know?"

"Well, there is one other thing I find bafflin', but it is what it is. You know about the 2030s when the implanted badge was real popular in Mother's Heartbeat?"

"Yes, I've seen them on a few grownups now. Is that what is so baffling?"

"Yeah. In the drug world, a device is very valuable if an addict has a badge implant. It makes for a very easy link up during a high. So adults who kept their implants since childhood, those be in the scene, always lookin' to link up with another user—in more ways than one, if you know what I mean."

"Did Torrone ever link up with a badge implant for the purpose of a high?"

"Well...actually, for several years, I been clean longer than Torrone, even, but I still been bad, Miss Chickee. I mean, I'm 'shamed to admit now, but I needed the money and 'badgers', as we call 'em, would pay rent to 'borrow' the device for a piggyback high. I made good money off it for awhile. Before I came to my senses. And well, before the doctor told me I'm dyin'...."

"What do you mean?" Chickee asked.

"Doctor says I got heart problems. My heart is turned to stone. Or on its way, anyhow. Cardiotrophy—Torrone has it too. Guess we be payin' for all we done wrong, huh?

"Mornin's are better. I get real tired and start coughin' and can't catch my breath by midday. I'm surprised I been talkin' your ears off. Usually I's outta breath before this. Guess my heart realizes I just gotta get it all said before it's too late."

"Well, that's something we haven't heard before, about the cardiotrophy. I appreciate you sharing, Delta. Like I said, the more we know, the better we can make the program." Chickee wanted to ask her even more questions, but sensed she was getting very tired at this point. "Can I please ask you a few more questions? I know you must be worn out by now."

"Yes, a little, and my kids are getting' restless out there. But they can wait. I reckon we oughtta do while we got a chance. You got me here right now, let's do it."

"Thank you, Delta. What I wonder is, is there a way to track down others with experiences like yours? We really need to document more of the effects of adult to adult linking, so we can get the word out to the public. Maybe more will avoid the black market use of the old devices if they realize how severe the consequences are."

"That's a question for Torrone, I s'pose, Chickee. He might not want to talk. We can ask him, though. I can explain the good it would do for you to know the most info possible from other link ups." She opened the door and the older man rushed over to give her a hand out of the car.

"Torrone," she began, "Chickee here need to talk to you, too."

"Oh, no—hell no," said Torrone quickly in a deep firm voice. His voice didn't match his physical appearance, thought Chickee.

"Torrone, you listen to me," continued Delta, "We got to do this for her. She's not goin' to place blame or put you in jail. She just wanna talk a minute about some of the people you know used the device."

Chickee chimed in at this point, since it seemed Torrone was at least willing to *listen*, if not share any info. "Whatever we learn now about how devices were used or misused helps us further out efforts later, hopefully to help more people. Whatever you can share, or whomever you can put me in touch with who'd be willing to share, I'd really appreciate it."

"I dunno. Some people might not want me spreadin' they name and phone number around, if you know what I mean."

"Yes, I understand. I would be very discreet. I could contact those with implant badges, for example, as if I'm doing a survey to gather support, for their experiences." Chickee could see this developing into a full-fledged research project. Exactly the thing Jared would have latched onto and gotten excited about. She really missed him in moments like this, even though it'd been thirty years since he died, and probably fifteen since she'd even "talked" to him in her own way.

"...I can't make any promises, but I'll talk to a couple dudes. See what we can drag up."

"That will be really helpful, Torrone, thank you. Is there anything from your personal experiences you could share, for the sake of research?"

"I dunno. I heard about this one dude, back when I was real young, he used it when he was, you know, in bed with his woman. He said it made the orgasm so intense. But I was too afraid of what might happen to ever try it. I figured my willy'd fall off, or it'd make me sterile. Neither sounded worth the risk."

Chickee diligently wrote down in her electric notebook all he said, keeping her chuckles to herself. Who knows what could have happened to those who abused it in that way. Maybe, just maybe, she would get to find out, if research efforts were fruitful. "Do you know what happened to the women in those kinds of situations? Did they enjoy it as well, or as much?"

Torrone shifted on his feet uncomfortably as he stood in the open doorway of the vehicle. "Um, well, I know they got the awful after headaches, same as what Momma got when she would link with somebody. I know that 'cause one guy was sayin' how 'at least she gets a headache *afterwards* and complains, instead of before and won't do anything 'cause "I got a headache tonight, honey."' The last part he mimicked in a sing song voice as if he was a headachy whiney wife or girlfriend.

"You've been a real help to me, Torrone. Both of you. Thank you. Is there anything else you can add? I really appreciate your time and honesty in this. It's crazy how we've been doing this for—how many years?—sixty years, and yet we still know so little..." Chickee said this last sentence almost to herself, pondering over why they hadn't tried to learn more sooner.

"There is one more thing, Miss Chickee," said Torrone in an afterthought. "One guy you wanna avoid is Chief. Big tall dude. He's named for his tattoo on his chest. He's just plain mean. If your contacts lead you to him, just walk away. Don' even call him. He's bad news."

"Thanks for the heads up." In some ways, she was doubtful she would have such success, she would have to *limit* whom she talked to for information on linking experiences.

Chapter Twenty-Eight

Research & Follow Up

2077

Chickee was now in research mode. Torrone called her within the week, offering a couple of names for a starting point. If the people said it was okay. Chickee didn't know what to expect from any of this, so she told herself she simply needed to learn whatever a person was willing to tell her.

She scaled down her linking appointments to one per week, and went on treks searching for past clients, friends of clients, counselors who might know how to contact them. Of course for privacy purposes, she could not actually get their info. She left her own contact info and hoped they would get in touch with her.

Several months went by, and Chickee spent hours poring over the old files she had stored up in her attic from the early years of Mother's Heartbeat. She meticulously investigated every thumb drive they had in each file, with hopes of contacting someone who would be willing to share what they knew about linking. She wanted to try to get ahold of every contact possible who might have had an implant, either of the nodule sort, or of the remote sort, similar to what Sonia had had. Finally, one day the phone rang, and she wasn't really expecting a stranger on the other end of the phone, but the person who answered when she replied hello said to her, "Is this Chickee Lane? I'm Treena and I was sent a letter regarding my remote implant. Are you the person I'm supposed to speak with?"

"Hello. Yes, this is Chickee Lane. Thank you for calling. I appreciate you getting back with me. I would like to survey you on your experience with Mother's Heartbeat and the record of your linking sessions with us. Would you be willing to answer some questions about that, and other questions about your implant?"

"Well, yes, I think so. Is that something we do over the phone, or did you want to meet in person?"

"Well, I would actually like to meet in person if we could. What city are you in?"

"Moberly, Missouri."

"Well, we could meet in Columbia quite easily. I live near there. Let's say we meet at the Denny's in Columbia? What would be a good time?"

"I'm available today or tomorrow, any time before six pm."

"Why don't we make it three-thirty tomorrow afternoon? We can have an ice tea or something. I really appreciate you getting back with me. I'll see you tomorrow."

In the springtime when the redbuds were blooming, Chickee found it easier to breathe, and she wondered to herself how many years she might actually have left. Today was the day she was going to meet up with Treena, someone she had sent a letter to about their nodule implant. This person was a child at the time of her implant, and would be probably in her forties or fifties at this point.

As she rode in the back, for she didn't do any driving anymore, she looked at all the flowers in other people's yards. All the colors and shapes and textures made her wish she had been an artist, or maybe an art therapist. She had always been one to help people, and she probably wouldn't have been able to survive without being interactive with people in some way. Artists always seemed such reclusive types. Yes, art therapy, maybe. Not that she had any regrets. Mother's Heartbeat had always been a success at different levels and different stages of Chickee's life. But now things were changing. Things were becoming less personally involved, and well, the word said it: remote. It was as if a person didn't have to have the interaction in order to accomplish the same things Mother's Heartbeat originally aimed to accomplish—creating that personal connection, and offering a child that nurturing sense of a prenatal relationship that causes such high amounts of growth and development at the cellular level in the healing stages. Due to all of the abuse and misuse, though, the devices that actually allowed a person to have contact in the process of linking had virtually been made obsolete and now the most chosen form of linking was remote access via a code.

Nowadays, every remote access device had the safeguards that Sarah Tinker had first suggested back in the late 2040s. There was a GPS tracker with a time and date stamp for every link up that occurred. Additionally, it recorded where the link up occurred. Finally, each Linker had a specific access code, their personal code that no one else should know or ever use, so it was known exactly who was using the device to do a linking every time it was used. Additional safeguards were a block on other electronic devices interfering with the linking, because that would diminish the effectiveness of the linking between the mother Linker and the child patient.

Although Chickee had been frustrated with the small number of inquiries from the files of the early days of Mother's Heartbeat, every time she went to an interview, she was surprised at how aged the people looked. This made her wonder if maybe the linking for them as a child pulled their years away from them, and in a sense, gave them to the Linkers. In addition, she was of course, wondering how many of them who said they had no adult linking experiences were being completely honest with her, because their bodies seemed older than their years.

Treena was one who was like this: old before her time.

"Tell me about your first linking experience, Treena."

"Well, I was the lucky one in the accident. I was only four years old. A drunk driver made a left turn into traffic and hit my babysitter's car in oncoming traffic. Neither of them survived. I had several broken bones and a cracked skull. I had a severe concussion, and was in intensive care for eight days. They gave me the implant right away, and I had several linking sessions during the year between my fourth and fifth birthdays. It was a long recovery."

"That was in 2037, which means now, in 2077, you are how old?" Chickee asked.

"Forty-six years old, but I look and feel almost twice that old!" complained Treena. Like Delta who was in her fifties, she looked like an elderly lady. She walked like an elderly lady; stooped over and frustratingly slow. She acted as though every move she made was painful for her body. And even her skin had not kept its youth.

They continued the interview. "Did you use tanning beds as a young person?"

"No."

"Do you, or have you ever been a smoker?"

"Yes, I smoked in my twenties. But after I found out I was pregnant with my first child, I quit. I never went back to it after that, thankfully."

"Were you ever involved in high risk or high contact sports, such as rock climbing, sky diving, wrestling, or long distance running or biking?"

All these factors mentioned in the interview could cause a person to age prematurely, and part of Chickee's goal was to address those issues. But Treena, it seemed, had not partaken in any of these alternative things that would cause a person to seem older than their years, so it was surprising how old she still looked.

"Have you used your implant nodule at any other time since your original accident and recovery?"

"No."

"Have you linked with anyone in any way other than the original reason you received the implant?"

"No." Treena stuck to her story and never admitted to using the nodule to link up as an adult, no matter how the questions were worded. "Can I ask you some questions, now, too?" she requested.

"Sure," replied Chickee.

"Okay, why do you look so young? Weren't you one of the *original* Linkers?"

"Over the years, we have discovered the linking process keeps a mother Linker young. But we've also found when adults link with other adults, the opposite occurs—people age prematurely."

"So, forgive me, but if I do the math in my head, you must be over a hundred years old; how can that be? You seem younger than my actual age in years! So, is that why I feel so old? Did you steal all my years away? Did whoever linked with me as a child deplete my store of youth?"

"That's a valid question, but one are not certain of the answer yet. That is part of what we are trying to figure out through these interviews, and the more information on linking experiences, child or adult, you could describe for us, the more thorough our research will be." She knew Treena wasn't satisfied with this answer, but it was all she could offer.

After a few more questions and recorded observations, it was the end of their conversation, and both ladies left the afternoon meeting with a sense of unresolved wonderings.

Chapter Twenty-Nine

Hovercraft Vehicles

2092

Chickee hadn't driven in about nineteen years, although she'd only come to Green Valley three years ago. (It seemed her body was finally going to slowly give out after all.) But her decision to quit driving was two-fold. Not only did her sight seem to fail her more often lately, but the driving format changed drastically. Until 2070, the hover craft vehicles (HCVs) generally followed the regular highways of the tire tread days, and were still "driven" by a person. In 2070, new transportation guidelines were issued, and hover craft vehicles were transformed to travel following a beacon toward a determined destination that a person would preprogram into the onboard computer. A person could override the auto pilot function if needed. Chickee went through the training for this new driving format at age 98, but the instructor deemed her unfit for behind-the-wheel activity due to her sight and hearing. Although she had always attempted to roll with the punches when it came to new technologies, she was not too keen on giving up total control to the machine anyway, so it seemed a blessing in disguise that the Motor Vehicle Department did not renew her driver's license.

The transition to relying on other people for transportation was less difficult than she expected it to be. At her age, she didn't have many places to go. The nice ladies at church always came by to pick her up for worship services. Her sister's great grandson graciously did her grocery shopping for her twice a month, and the hairdresser always came to her house, so she didn't have a great need to drive on a daily basis anyway. It was more of a pride thing to give up her driver's license. After all, she had had one since September 23, 1988, the day she turned sixteen. That was eighty-eight years! Most people are lucky if they *live* that long, even with the life expectancy rates steadily rising due to the many wonderful medical advancements of recent years.

One of the greatest advancements in technology was the voice recognition software that came standard on all personal communication devices. Not only did Chickee no longer need to remember three dozen different passwords, (she couldn't have anyway; her memory seemed to be growing smaller as time went by), but the voice recognition would also type in the words for her when she wanted to write something down. She could easily create her grocery list for Terrence (her great grandnephew) simply by talking to her PCD.

It was time for another meal. *Didn't we just eat? thought Chickee to herself.* The man who reminded her of Wilson sat at her table tonight. She couldn't think of his name. She wondered what the color of the day would be. Tara set a tray in front of her that looked orange. *Yay! Orange!* she thought. Orange breaded chicken patty. Sliced carrots, cooked nearly to orange mush. Mandarin oranges in a little styro cup. Butterscotch pudding—also orangish—in a little puddle next to the carrots. Instead of the orange conglomeration in front of her, Chickee stared at the man across the table who reminded her of Wilson. Dark, thick hair, dark sparkling eyes and a mischievous smile on a square face and a once stocky, muscular body. Wilson was one of Chickee's closest friends in college. They never dated, but were more like brother and sister. She recalled the night Wilson called her, desperate for a connection with a friend during a difficult time.

"Hey, I need to talk to a friend. I really need someone to pray for me. I am going through a really rough spot and I need to talk."

"Sure. Of course. You know I'm always here. What's up?"

"Well, she asked me to leave. I've been out of the house for about a month and it's killing me. I haven't seen the kids in two weeks. I can't believe this is happening." He told Chickee of the struggles they'd been having, and how he's been trying to make some changes in himself; praying his wife will be forgiving and willing to make some changes herself.

After getting several details and sympathizing with his situation, Chickee told him, "One thing I do know: every every EVERY marriage can be saved, if the two people in the relationship are willing to do what they need to do to turn back to God."

"Thank you. Thank you for being a good friend."

Chapter Thirty

Forced

2086

One particularly cold and dreary fall day, Chickee woke late and decided to stay home, when unexpectedly, the doorbell rang. She was surprised, answering the door in her robe, and was suddenly more awake, when a big tall bulky man shoved himself inside. "Where is it? Where are you hiding it? Get it out now!" he demanded with a scowl.

"What? What? I don't know what you're talking about!"

"Your linking device! Go get it!" he shouted. He frightened her with his loud voice. His angry dark eyes pierced her with pure evil. He looked as though he needed a shave. He had on sweatpants and black shoes. They were wet and muddy; like he'd been running through puddles. They were splattered with white spots, already crusted over with dried mud. Startled to alertness, she heard the gun click to cocked, and saw it protruded at her from inside his hoodie pocket.

"Um, h-hold on...Just a moment. G-give me a chance to pull myself together. You don't have to be so r-rude." She tightens her robe belt around her waist and tucks in the top to cover herself better.

"I'm not here to wait on you or be nice. Go-Get-It-Bitch!"

She went into her room and pulled it out of the back of her closet. He follows closely behind her, his big muddy shoes pounding the floor like the thump of her heart in her chest. It was still in that same KROGER's bag Delta had given it to her in several years ago. Even the belt and the metal plate Delta had talked about were in the bag with the linking device. She had checked it in with the Mother's Heartbeat Headquarters, but since it was not a subdermal or remote device, it was so old it would have been discarded, so she took it home and stashed it away. Chickee really didn't have an occasion to need or use it since then. She didn't truly grasp the fear of the moment yet. She thought she was being robbed. As they walked back into the living room with his too close hoodie pocket poking her, and his two cruel eyes piercing her, she began to shiver and shakily handed him the bag. "There. Now get out!"

"Oooo no. I'm not goin' nowheres. I'm taking a turn with you! Hook us up!" He was getting impatient. He wrestled out of his hoodie, then pulled his dirty T-shirt off over his head.

She was gulping back tears of fear as she realized he wants more than just the device. *Oh God, I'm just an old lady. He doesn't want me!* The bluish black tattoo that covered his barrel of a chest was a Native American headdress: CHIEF!

"You hook me up and help get this cancer outta me now! I know you can do it. Hurry up!"

Oh, he doesn't desire *me. He wants healing.* "B-but it doesn't work that w-way." She tried to explain. "W-with an a-a-adult, it's—it's not the same!"

"You healed all them children, right? It's my turn for some healing. Now hook us up!"

Chickee looked at the bulk of the man and thought, *that belt isn't going to fit around his barrel chest!* But her mouth didn't form the words. Her hands trembled as she attempted to hook up the Velcro wrist band to her own arm, and she saw from her fumbling fingers, she visibly trembled.

"Hurry up! What are you waiting for, bitch? I ain't got all the time in the world, here!"

"P-please, be patient. I'm working on it." She heard the fear in her voice, even though her words sounded tough. She couldn't really believe this was happening. She had heard of times when Linkers were forced to link against their will, but it had certainly never happened to her. In all her one hundred plus years, she had never felt so violated. She could not believe someone would use something so good for so vile a purpose.

Her thoughts jumped all around. No surprise, they jumped straight to her dear Jared. She wished he was still here. He was the one to always keep a gun in the house, and keep a watchful eye on things. But when he died, Chickee wasn't comfortable keeping a gun in the house. She was afraid an intruder would be able to take it from her and use it against her. So she got rid of his guns; gave them all to Reece. Heaven only knows what Reece did with them. But now she felt defenseless.

After she had the Velcro wrist band attached and shakily reattached the connection to the belt, he grabbed her hands and forced them behind her back. "This w-works better if you are not constricted," she tried to argue.

"Shut up, bitch!" He tied her hands together behind her back with the cord from the table lamp; it dug into her skin. She worried it would tangle with the device tether. But she gave up saying anything to him. Tears trickled down her cheeks unrestricted. He pushed her to the floor and straddled her to hold her down. She could hardly breathe. He attempted to strap the belt around himself. As she wriggled to adjust, she felt like her shoulders were going to pop out of socket with her hands behind her back like that and all his weight bearing down on her chest. She squeezed her eyes tight and tears dripped down each side of her face. *Is this going to be how I go? I don't want this to be how I die!*

Chickee watched with big scared eyes as he struggled to buckle the last hole shut. He was a big man. She could barely breathe with the weight of him on her. She squeezed silent tears out of the sides of her eyes and felt them make paths down the sides of her face into her ears. The whole time he muttered to himself, cussing up a storm and getting angrier and angrier as things didn't go the way he thought they should.

Chickee wondered what sort of plan he had. He must be misguided about linking. She refused to believe he wanted to use the device for a sexual escapade with her. Yes, she was young-looking for her age, but she still looked like an older woman, maybe not a one hundred-fifteen year old woman... Did he have drugs with him? He couldn't know the effects of adult-to-adult linking or he wouldn't be forcing her to do this!

"What's your plan?" she croaked. "Do you know what you're getting into here?"

"Shut up. Just shut up. I know what I'm doin'. You think I dunno? I know you're gonna be the one with a headache later and I'm gonna be better. You just do your part and I won't kill you."

When he said this, Chickee saw his face flash a brief change from anger when he realized where his gun actually was—in his hoody pocket over by the front door. He looked over toward the door and visibly debated whether or not to get up and go get it. The determined look on his face returned and showed her he was resigned to do this without it. Not that Chickee could have taken him even without a weapon. He was much bigger and stronger than she was and she knew better than to get herself killed for resisting.

Truthfully, she had been so afraid, she had not even realized he didn't have his gun nearby. If she had thought of it first, she might have tried to get it and shoot him and run.

She felt like a coward for not trying to get herself out of this predicament, but she didn't know what she could do. She felt like maybe if she cooperated, she might live to ID the guy and get him convicted. So instead, she concentrated on memorizing details about him that would help her identify him to the police.

She dared to ask him another question. "How'd you know I've got a linking device?"

"What do you mean, how did I know? Everybody knows you're the heartbeat lady. And then you go leavin' business cards everywhere, sayin' contact you about linking experiences. I just put two and two together and got four.

"And now you're gonna show me how it's done. I wanna feel good. I'm so tired of feelin' sick and tired. Doctors tell me I got a tumor. You're gonna help me shrink it."

"What makes you think I can do that?"

"You help all them kids get well, right? Well, now it's my turn. Help me." It was a command, not a plea.

"You're gonna be disappointed in what you get," she warned him, trying to remain as calm as possible, "This works differently when it's adult-to-adult. It ends up working like a slow draining battery. It will drain me, but it will drain you, too. Is that what you want?"

"I don't believe you. You're just tryin' to keep me from using your device. I'm not listenin' to you. We're gonna do this my way. Now let's go!"

And he flipped the switch on the device.

Chickee thought she was going to choke. She felt smothered, like a dark veil was crawling slowly over her entire body until she couldn't see or feel anything. As the blackness crept up on her, her life force slowly drained away. Darkness.

She distantly heard him catch his breath and cry out, like someone was stabbing him in the chest. She fought to catch her own breath, and only when he spasmed and thudded to the floor next to her, did she feel like she could catch her breath a little, only in tiny wisps at first.

She laid there for a long time, unable to move or think. At last, the darkness over her began to fade. Her head pounded and she felt the familiar thirst. She wriggled to get her hands free, but the cords seemed to tangle the more she struggled to get her hands undone.

When she looked around, she could see that the belt had busted off his chest, and the link had been broken. Thankfully. But he was nowhere to be seen.

She looked around desperately trying to locate her PCD and call 911, but her head was foggy and it pounded like a hammer on metal, she couldn't remember where she had laid it down.

Looking to her left, she saw the familiar shiny cover on the entryway table. Was that her PCD lying up there? She tried to move over in that direction. If she could just wake it up, she could voice dial some help. It was slow and difficult because every move she made caused her head to throb worse. She dragged the lamp in tow, still attached to the cord that bound her hands. She was dragging the belt as well, for it was still attached to the wire of her wrist band device. While she tried with her bare feet to pull herself closer to the entryway table, she was frustrated with her robe, which had bunched up behind her from the sliding. It further tangled her hands in the cords behind her and she groaned as it slowed her down.

She was almost close enough to kick at the little table when her doorbell rang. Then a knock-knock on the door. "Chickee?

Are you home?" The person tried the door and it was unlatched. "Oh no! Chickee!" Her helpful neighbor, Edward, rushed in to assist her.

Her robe was splayed open, and her nightgown up around her waist from the scooting along the floor. She was embarrassed, but it couldn't be helped. Edward respectfully pulled the two halves of her robe over her body as best he could, and then worked to untangle her from the lamp cord, the device wires, and the belt straggling along behind. "Just a moment," he mumbled. "Let me help you with this." He didn't look her in the eyes. "Are you okay?" He continued talking without waiting for Chickee to answer.

"I was just coming to ask if you needed anything from the store," Edward explained himself nervously. "I never expected...." But he didn't finish his sentence.

Chickee rubbed her wrists after she removed the Velcro wrist band, and reached for her phone as she tried to express thanks to Edward. He was at a loss for words, so he waited for her to speak. But when the 911 dispatcher asked her what her emergency was, she burst into inconsolable sobs. Edward took the phone with a compassionate look on his face, explained there had been a break in, and gave the address.

Edward got Chickee a glass of water for her thirst, and was warming up water for tea in the microwave when they heard the sirens announce the arrival of help. The ambulance crew insisted on taking Chickee to the hospital, to have everything checked out, even though she told them she was okay. Her head hurt so badly, she didn't really protest; but she might have if she'd known how long it would take.

Six hours later, she called Bridgette to take her home. The hospital staff who had released her recommended she see a counselor and process what she had been through, but Chickee dismissed that idea. She was more interested in identifying the guy who did this, and quietly determined she would get to the police department and follow up with more details the next day. Right now, she was still in a fog.

"Are you sure you're gonna be alright?" Bridgette asked when they got back to Chickee's house. "You could come stay the night at our house, you know. Malcolm and Theo won't mind." Theo was their second child. Ellie had already gone off to college the year before last. "You could stay in Ellie's room for a night or two."

"No, no. I'll be fine," she insisted. She sounded like she was trying to convince herself as much as she was Bridgette. She saw the lamp lying there on the floor in the entryway, the primary casualty of the day. And there was her linking device, all strewn out from being dragged behind her as she had painstakingly worked her way to the entryway table.

Bridgette leaned down to pick it all up. "Let me take this and get it all cleaned up and checked out for you, Chickee."

"No thanks. That's okay. I'm going to put it back in its bag here," she leaned over and picked up the KROGER bag, "and put it away for now. I won't be needing it anyway."

Bridgette could see by the look on her face that she was still fighting off an awful after-headache.

"Chickee, why don't you drink a big glass of water and take a couple of Tylenol, and go to bed for tonight. Headaches are so thirsty, you know."

"Bridgette, I think you're probably right. I need to sleep off this headache before I try to do anything else." She followed Bridgette's recommendations, and the sweet girl stayed long enough to see that Chickee was tucked warmly in bed and relaxing.

Chapter Thirty-One

Drained

2086

Getting out of bed was hard the next day, and the next day after that, too. It was like the intruder had not only drained her body physically, but it was soon evident that he had drained all the life out of the woman, too. She found no joy in things anymore. Finally, she knew she had to go down to the police station and make her report. She described the guy and all the details she could remember of the incident. She prayed they would find him and convict him.

She refused to get back on the linking schedule at the hospital. Linking almost seemed repulsive to her now. This personal tragedy she had survived had been all but the death of her. Some days she thought death would have been better than living through it. The feeling that she had been electronically raped took more than her physical strength. It had robbed her of the *good* in her life and left her feeling empty and violated.

Chickee had bad dreams at night. She would wake up tangled in the bed linens and feeling like she was bound and gagged. Her head hurt. Her thirst was insatiable. It was like she couldn't recover from that last linking after-headache.

And she couldn't. She knew she would not link up with children anymore. This had taken her joy out of linking and she didn't even want to try it again to get it back.

2087

After several months of just *existing*, Chickee realized she was not going to feel better about this, ever, not as long as she lived on her own and in this house. Even though this house held many memories of Jared, she made the decision to sell the house. The ugly memory of the forced link up overshadowed all the good memories of the house now.

She sold most of her things by auction, bringing in someone to do all the work, and she used her funds and her retirement account to fund a spot at Green Valley Nursing Center. She figured with her age, they wouldn't have any problem admitting her, and it would make life easier, not having to worry about meals, or housekeeping, or any of the everyday chores anymore. She could *rest.*

Chapter Thirty-Two

So Many Goodbyes

2060

After giving up linking, Chickee spent a lot of time daydreaming about the people she had lost through the many years of her long life. She spent many hours crying over Jared, Sherry, Sonia, Todd, Joan; even Sean.

They tried to make the best of the weekend in South Padre Island, after the linking devices were stolen that Friday in Galveston. Although they had a wonderful time together, and reminisced about all the good times they had in college, both of them became aware that the friendship was not going to become a serious commitment. It seemed after losing their spouses, they could neither one capture a "true love" feeling for another. Although they still shared a sort of kindred connection, neither Sean nor Chickee was ready for another eventual heartbreak like the first one. They agreed their friendship was special, and they continued to keep in touch online, less and less over time, until the only communication was an occasional holiday greeting. Nonetheless, when she read the posting from Sean's granddaughter that he had passed peacefully in his sleep, she wept in sadness for the loss. She attended his funeral in Tulsa, and imagined most of the people at the service wondered who she was.

But the one loss that made her cry now was Todd.

2053

His eyes were friendly. Immediately she realized he was a charming, amiable, approachable person who probably didn't know a stranger. When he walked by her as she sat in the booth of the Dairy Queen, he smelled like fresh aloe lotion. He sat down with his tray in a booth where she could still see him from where she sat. When he caught her eye, he smiled very openly. She noticed he had a red nose, and surprisingly smooth skin for his age; she imagined he must be in his upper sixties. His hair was bright white, and neatly combed so you could see the rows of comb like a plowed white field on his head.

As she munched on her chicken tenders, the more she looked at the man, the more familiar he seemed. He continued to smile at her and make eye contact as if he knew her, too. Suddenly she recognized those eyes! No, it couldn't be!

"Todd?"

"Hi Chickee. I wondered how long it might take you to recognize me."

"Oh, wow! I can't believe it's you! Tell me how life has treated you. It's so good to see you!" She silently did some math in her head. Todd would only be in his fifties now. She wondered to herself if linking had prematurely aged him as well, even as a child patient.

"Yes, you too. Well, I'm a retired train conductor. You remember how much I loved trains? Well, I made a living at it for thirty years. My ex-wife didn't like being left alone so much though. She and my daughter live in Chicago now. My daughter, Clarissa is a teacher in an upper class district there. She loves it." He pulled his PCD out of his shirt pocket and made a few clicks to a collections of pictures. "Here's Clarissa."

"She's beautiful. She has your eyes," Chickee complimented sincerely. She couldn't believe the luck. She had often wondered what became of Todd. Once he was declared cancer-free, and formally adopted by his foster parents, they moved away from Missouri and had lost touch for the last forty years. "I can't believe the luck! What brought you back to Missouri?"

"Well, truthfully, darn the luck, that," Todd joked. "I'm afraid the monster has returned. I am about to begin my treatments this week."

"Oh, Todd, I'm so sorry to hear that. And doubly sorry I can't link with you—perhaps you've heard of the few adult-to-adult linkings we know about; to say the least, they've not gone well. It's not something Mother's Heartbeat endorses."

"That's okay, Chickee. You've already done so much for me, and I'm grateful. I'm grateful for all these many years I've enjoyed, and hey! I'm not dead yet; I've got a fight ahead of me. And not like I don't even know what to expect, right?"

"Right." She tried to stay positive. "So give me your contact info while you're here and I'll send you a message so you'll have mine. That way, we can keep in touch."

Tears streamed down Chickee's face as she remembered Todd. That happy reunion in the Dairy Queen, but the heartbreaking funeral she attended only a year after that. He didn't survive the second fight. Everything seemed so pointless. She felt so useless, so hopeless. Everybody she has ever loved is going to die and she is going to feel that grief over and over again. It was too much for her heart to bear.

Chapter Thirty-Three

The Lonely Tree

2087

Life at Green Valley was very social and the atmosphere distracted her from her misery. The violation had sucked all the good out of life for her. Things that used to bring her joy, now seemed to elude her. At the end of the hallway in Green Valley, there was a large window looking out over a green field, with a lone tree standing defiantly.

When Chickee first came to Green Valley, she would walk to the end of the hallway and stand there staring at that lonely tree. It reminded her of herself; she wondered if it was ever lonely or afraid. At least she didn't have to be so afraid living here with all these other people.

And how entertaining they all were. A welcome distraction became people-watching. Darlene was her roommate. Murphy, Sal, and Gus usually flirted with her at dinnertime, and flattered her at every opportunity, as if they were competing for her attention. Grumpy Pete muttered his continual discontentment about something. And Dina, the sweet, childlike lady who carried around a teddy bear in her purse, was always ready to go on the resident van for a ride. It didn't matter where it was going; she was ready to "go to town."

In some ways, Chickee related to Darlene, too. Darlene was the one who was afraid. She was childlike in a different way. She was afraid of the dark. She was afraid of being alone. And she was afraid of going to hell.

"You're not going to hell, Darlene," the night nurse reassured her. "Just rest easy, honey. Have sweet dreams." Chickee pretended the nurse was speaking to her, and she reminded herself to 'have sweet dreams.' Often, though, she woke up in a sweat with her heart pounding and the covers all tangled up. Sometimes she stayed up at night to avoid the dreams, and napped during the day in her easy chair.

Time passed by in Green Valley without any awareness. Meals, baths, bedtime, naptime. TV time, visitors. She particularly liked visitors. Reece came on her birthday, and on every holiday, but she was lonesome for him in the in-between times. Bridgette visited periodically too, and always made her day.

When other residents had visitors, everyone seemed to perk up and want to make conversation with the different faces. They were always cordial and smiling, but somewhat reserved and uncomfortable, too. Chickee recognized visitors were ready to leave the home after a short while. She knew it must be depressing for family members to see their loved ones so old and weary and decrepit. She wondered sometimes what her own visitors thought when they came to see her.

Sometimes remembering the past was the best way to spend the time. She tried to remember the happy times, like when Reece was little, or when they went on a family trip to Branson. But it seemed like sometimes she couldn't keep the sad memories at bay. They popped up without her permission and made for a weepy day.

Chapter Thirty-Four

An Idea Forms

2092

Chickee still had a wristband version of the linking system. She had stowed it away when the hacking grew rampant. She had insisted on taking it with her to Green Valley when she finally moved out of her home.

In the 2030's, since the wristband device was the easiest way to link without a code or PCD, they were being stolen right and left when thrill seekers realized the wristband version did not need special training or information to simply transmit a signal. Drug users could get twice the thrill for twice the people on half the crack by using a linking device while one of them was high. By the time users figured out it was possible, Dr. Newburg had developed the first remote implants, like the one Sonia required, so the wristband devices were being stored away or discarded. A few were even sold at garage sales, and those were the hardest ones to track down when the authorities started putting a pinch on the misuse of devices.

Chickee held onto a couple of the old versions because she liked them so much better. Even though they only had a five-foot tether of wire, she felt like they provided a clearer, more consistent link to the patient. Even when a child had an implant, she preferred to use the wristband/skin electrode sticker mode of linking, so she always carried one with her in her car. During the years she still drove, that is. Here at Green Valley, she hadn't had an occasion to use it, but the thought did occur to her maybe she could help some of these folks make a *transition.* Was she really considering linking again, after what happened? Was she willing to risk shortening her own life to help them out? Well, that one was easy. She's already had twice the life most people get. But what about the headaches? Especially since she knew from experience the after headache was even worse when linking with an adult rather than a child. Not to mention the mental frailty factor.

She tried to think about what Jared might say about this idea. Chickee formulated the imaginary conversation in her mind.

"I want to help the old folks here in their transition from Life to Death."

"You always have had a very tender heart for helping people. Are you sure you're willing to go through all the side effects of linking with adults?"

"Yeah, I know. I thought about that. But Jared, I haven't felt that deep sense of satisfaction from really helping someone out since I last linked regularly with patients. That's been since the incident..."

"Chickee, look at the life you've led. I can't imagine you aren't satisfied with it. Why do you need more?"

"Maybe in a way I feel like this is my final gift to others. I mean, seven years ago, for me, the end of linking was very sudden and traumatic. I want to do it my way. I want to 'go out with a bang,' you know?"

"Of course, linking may speed that going out a bit, shortening what time you have left." Jared always had a way of looking at things realistically. "Is that something you're willing to risk? And what about all those headaches?"

"I think I'll feel more *alive* if I'm helping people again. The one thing I think about in shortening my time is that it will be much sooner I will get to see you again." Although it was mostly a thought conversation, a real lump in her throat still formed.

"I'm always here when you need me, Sweetie. I'll always love you, more than anything."

"I love you, Jared. I miss you, too. So much."

Chickee knew Jared could help her decide.

The afternoon activity was a group of singers and a piano player the size of Texas. She had a beautiful voice. They all did. It must be Sunday. Sundays were when the people came to sing. This group was especially lively; they even brought their own sound system. That meant their sound would resonate even to the rooms down the hall. If you can't avoid it, might as well join it, thought Chickee. She sat and scanned the room for whom she might help first.

Chapter Thirty-Five

Patient Identified

2092

It occurred to her she was wagering on the near death of someone in the room, and the thought startled her about herself. In a way, she was *hopeful* for it, for the opportunity to link again. It was a little bit morbid to think about, so she tried to focus on the singing instead.

"In the sweeeet by and by, we will meet on that beautiful shore. In the sweeeet by and by, we will meet on that beautiful shore."

Even the songs were about the transition from life into death. Chickee took that as a sign. She would roam the halls and peek into rooms for somebody bedridden instead. The music would be loud enough; she could enjoy it on her stroll as well as standing here at the back of the room.

She thought about Murphy, a man who came to Green Valley the same day she did. She remembered him because when he got here, he was a drugged up, slobbering fool. After two weeks starting him back at square one, the medical staff had created a work horse. He would roam the halls day and night. He would attempt to fix anything that had a screw in it, whether it was broken or not. He imagined he carried around a tool box wherever he went, and got angry when he couldn't find it. He was sure someone had stolen it, and he would report to the nurses as if they were the police.

About nine months into his stay, Murphy quit roaming. He started sitting in front of the TV in the gathering room. He would carry on conversations with people onscreen and get grumpy when someone changed the channel. As time went on, he quit paying attention to the TV, and snoozed a lot. Then he started only showing up at mealtimes. He would eat at Chickee's table sometimes, but he never made conversation more than one or two word answers if she asked him a question.

Recently, Chickee hadn't seen him in the gathering room at all, so in the back of her mind, she hoped she would figure out which room was his. Down at the end of the West hallway, the sun shone in and made a glare on the floor. Chickee decided to look out the window for a moment, and set aside her task for the chance to feel the late afternoon sun shine on her face. The sun was still bright enough, it made her want to close her eyes. It warmed her skin and she shut her eyes to soak it in for a moment. But she resolutely opened them again. She stood at the window, and looked out over a field of grass. There was one lonely tree about twenty feet from the building and a few twittering birds flitted ground to branch and back again. Chickee tried to spot a nest somewhere in the tree, but the foliage was thick in the warm spring air, so it was already well hidden. She heard the singing group in the gathering room, with the tinkling sound of the piano along for the ride. "Count your blessings, name them one by one. Count your blessings, see what God has done. Count your blessings. Name them one by one. Count your many blessings see what God has done."

Chickee counted her blessings. Top of the list: Reece. Jared. Life. Linking. Stella. Sunshine. Sight. Songs. Birds. Technology. She knew she could come up with a long list, but interrupting her thoughts, she heard a familiar voice call out, "Oooow," and she turned around to the hallway, remembering why she had come this direction.

"Murphy? It's Chickee."

A groan. "Ooooow," he mumbled again. She followed the sound, intuitively knowing she should help. Two doors down on the left, she peeked in and saw him lying half covered in bed, on his right side, so he was facing away from the doorway.

"Murphy?" The lights were off, but the blinds had not been completely drawn, and in the afternoon light Chickee could see his bony body, his pale and smooth skin, and his spine, jutted out like a line of sharp hills down his back. The rolling tray held a meal tray that looked mostly ignored. The sheet was rumpled around his waist and his wispy hair was gnarled and unkempt on the side of his head.

"Huh? Who's that? Ooooow, my bones ache."

"Murphy. I'm Chickee. Do you know who I am? We sat at dinner together sometimes. And we both like to watch that nature show, what's it called?"

"Nature….hmmm. Urmmmm." He rolled onto his back so he could see who was talking to him, and he tried to pull his cover up, but he only weakly fumbled for it. Chickee walked closer and helped him bring it up closer to his chin, covering his shoulders.

"Are you cold? Here, let me help you."

"Mmm. Thanks," he replied. It always surprised Chickee how old people would talk in as few words as possible, but most still remembered their manners.

"Hey, Murphy, I like to talk to you; can I come talk to you sometime? Would that be alright?" She didn't quite know how to broach the subject of linking with him. She decided she would try to become a familiar presence, and go from there. This might take a few visits to make him comfortable with her. "Would that be okay with you, Murphy?"

"Mmmm," he mumbled distantly. She sat on the chair next to his bed for a few moments as he fell back asleep.

She felt like she had made a start of it. Patient identified. Now she needed to get some rubbing alcohol. That might be a little bit of a challenge. Chickee had tried to keep some pain reliever and Band-aids in her nightstand when she first arrived at Green Valley, but the nurses swiped it up and put it in a locked room near their desk. It seemed anything belonging in a medicine cabinet stayed under tight lock and key around here.

Chapter Thirty-Six

Fellow Residents at Green Valley Nursing Center

2092

"Chickee? You have a phone call, sweetie," the new nurse (Chickee couldn't remember her name yet) brought her an oversized PCD and helped her strap it to her head where the earpiece and tiny microphone were positioned correctly.

"Hello?"

"Hi, Mom. How are you? Are they feeding you enough?"

"Hi, Reece. I'm good. Are you really worried your old mother would ever go hungry? The food's not the best, but nobody around here starves to death unless by choice. How was your trip?"

"Oh, good, Mom. I wanted to come show you the photos, but I got sidetracked helping Mrs. Goodall next door. She was out there all by herself trimming bushes with a small pair of hedge trimmers the other day. So I pulled out the electric trimmer and went to work on it. Then she asked me in for tea. Well, long story short, she and I have been spending time together. She's a nice lady. Did you know she's only seven years younger than me? I'm gonna take her to that new home style restaurant on 7th Street tomorrow night."

"Good, Reece. So you like her?"

"She's really funny, Mom. And pretty. Dad would've liked her, too. Can you believe me? Romantic interests at seventy-something years old!"

"Well, Sean and I got together at seventy-something. It's not so strange as you think. So when can I see those photos of your trip up North?"

"Well, I wanted to see if we could have lunch on Saturday, then we could go get some things from the store, and I could show you the pictures. How does that sound?"

"Oh, Reece. That's a great idea. How about 11 a.m.? Is that too early?"

"Nope. Mom, that sounds good. I'll see you then, 'kay? Love you, Mom."

"Yes, that sounds good. Love you, Reece. So glad you called, sweetie."

Chickee was excited to see her son on Saturday. And a little bit tickled to hear he had found a girl he was really interested in—and she was his next door neighbor for several years. Funny how these things happen.

Saturday would be the perfect opportunity to get a supply of cotton balls and alcohol for her plans. This would eliminate any need for her to rely on someone else. Would the authorities try to arrest her if they found out she *assisted* someone to pass over to the "other side?" She needed to visit Murphy today and see how he's doing. She was worried she might miss the window of opportunity for helping him make the transition.

Today was Thursday, according to the activities calendar in the gathering room. There was going to be a craft time this afternoon. It might be the best time for her to go visit Murphy undisturbed. First, there was lunch. She would have to look around more and see who might need her help in the next few months. She needed to be ready to link for transition at any time. She felt a little strange, almost wishing for people around her to be close to death. It was so ironic. The more she thought about her plan, the more she was convinced the only way for her to finally transition herself and end this longevity she had had so far was to link with adults and *deplete* her own life force. Would it work? She was hoping so. And also hoping in this effort, her last days, weeks, months, whatever it took, would be purposeful again, like back when she was linking regularly.

Chickee also thought it was strange how she didn't really

remember the miseries of linking, only the satisfaction of helping people. Whenever she thought about linking again, she didn't think about the excruciating headaches. She mostly thought about the children, their personalities, their hopefulness, and their fascination at how linking simply worked to help them heal. She didn't think about the horrible thirst a linking session left her with; instead, she remembered feeling like she'd done something good, something right.

Now, she knew she had to be able to focus even more. To allow herself to be the medium between life and death might be harder than she realized, but she was determined to try. She was willing to endure the pain, like before. Even though this pain might be quite a bit more tremendous than the post linking migraines she got from helping children. Her experience was that the after headache was much worse when linking with an adult. And there was the undeniable fact: linking with a mentally "touched" person caused difficulties. No doubt the residents here were "touched." Dementia was common in elderly folks, even more common now than it was when her own mother got so old and frail and wasn't always in touch with reality.

Lunch was a tuna sandwich and chips plus a little green Jello salad. Chickee sat across from Gus and Jake, with Darlene, her roommate, there too. They weren't nearly as flirtatious today. It was rather a relief, because she was scouting out the room. At the table next to theirs, she noticed Sal. Sal was a very weak, aged Mexican man who spoke with an accent. He spoke so little these days, it was amazing Chickee even knew this about him. But he had the olive skin, salt and pepper hair, and roundish face of a Mexican American. He had to have his meal as a plate of various purees in their own compartments. He had to have thickener put into his tea and juice in order to swallow it. He laid back on the reclining hover bed. The nursing assistant pressed a button that made it sit more upright so he could eat his meal. She spooned a bit of tuna mush into his mouth, and he feigned chewing motions, swallowed. Next, she spooned a bite of green gelatin up for him, and he used the same chewing motion, even though Jello doesn't require chewing.

At the table past Sal, Chickee watched a man named Pete. Pete was a grumpy fellow. He always had something to complain loudly about. Chickee suspected he was raised in an atmosphere of discontent; how else would someone be so completely unhappy with every little thing around him? Chickee suspected this was a learned behavior. She wondered if he was miserable, or if he was one of those people who thrived on being able to complain about every imperfection of Life. One thing she did know: his life would be shortened for all the negativity he exuded from himself.

One other person Chickee had her eye on was Darlene, her roommate. Darlene was in a hover chair and could barely move her arms and legs. She also was on a liquid diet, and hardly ever seemed to care much about her meals. She was a tiny lady with loose flabby skin hanging on her bones, as if she was once a very large woman with lots of soft flesh underneath that skin. She made pitiful noises when she was unhappy with something. *Poor Darlene*, thought Chickee. Darlene rarely talked, but when she did, she spoke of how afraid she was. "Are you afraid of the dark? I'm afraid of the dark." Her eyes got wide and round and sincere, and welled up with big fat tears. "I'm going to hell," she said. "I've done some bad things. Do you think I'm gonna go to hell?"

Charlotte, the night nurse, reassured her, "Darlene, you know you're not going to hell. Why would you even say such a thing? Tell me what heaven is gonna be like. That's what you need to be thinking about, girl." Yet Darlene still welled up in tears often, and worried away whole days.

Chickee ate about half her sandwich and chips and took a couple bites of green gelatin salad, but she had her mind on other things. If she could get the supplies when she went out on Saturday with Reece, perhaps she could attempt to link with Murphy on Saturday night. Only two and a half days away. She excused herself and left her napkin over her plate to hide how her meal wasn't really eaten. They watched very closely on these things here.

Down the hall towards Murphy's room, Chickee glanced again at the tree out the far window. It was full of spring green, and blowing gently in the breeze. She turned in to the door near the end of the hall, and said his name, "Murphy?"

"Uh?" Once again, his back was turned to the door. His covers were half hanging off the bed. Chickee walked in and pulled them up around his shoulders, tucking him in as she put her hand on his arm. He would need to be familiar with her touch for her to be able to hook him up without an incident, like a paranoid attack or an angry outburst, both common in Alzheimer's patients.

"It's me, Chickee." She went around the bed and looked at him. His face was scruffy, like it had been a few days since he'd had a shave. His white hair spun off in every direction, making him look disheveled and much like a neglected stray mutt. "How are you doing today, Murphy?" She used her fingers to comb his hair down as best she could.

He didn't answer, but opened his eyes momentarily and looked up at her with a uncertainty in his eyes. Slowly he closed them again. Chickee continued soothingly touching him, on his arm, his back, and his head, as if he were a small child sick in bed. He seemed upset when she touched his face, so she didn't do that anymore. She talked to him in a soft voice, "Can I tell you a story? Would you like that?" It was a story about an angel who held a little boy's hand as he walked across a bridge into a beautiful field of green grass. "In the field, a sweet golden retriever puppy ran and romped with the boy. He forgot all about the glowing angel and she faded away. The boy and the puppy played all day until they were tired and laid down in the soft grass, looking up at the sky and imagining shapes in the puffy white clouds. The puppy fell asleep at the boy's side. When they woke up, there was a fishing pole leaning against a tree, so they walked to the brook and cast a line in. It was the perfect day."

Murphy's face transformed into a smile, and although he didn't open his eyes, he asked Chickee, "Where is Steven?"

"Steven? He crossed the bridge to the other side."

"When? Why did he go? I want to go there, too."

"Who is Steven? Is he your son?" she prodded a little.

"My brother, Steven. He was twelve when the puppy ran into the road..." Suddenly Murphy was crying, tears falling sideways down his face as he laid there remembering. "The big truck couldn't stop in time. How did you know?"

"Steven's okay now, Murphy." She took a leap of faith with the next sentence. "He's waiting for you, you know."

"Steven? I'll be there soon. Tired. Need to go lay in the grass."

"Yes, you'll go lay in the grass too. I'll come back soon, Murphy. You rest now."

Chapter Thirty-Seven

Fish Scale

2092

Chickee was trying to figure out how she was going to get ahold of some rubbing alcohol. At dinner the next night—a yellow meal this time, with cream corn (blech!), little peach squares, a breaded chicken patty, and lemon pudding—Chickee noticed something interesting about James as he leaned over Gus across the table from her to arrange his drink and napkin for him. James had a receptor nodule. His nurse smock gaped at the neck and revealed this to her, along with a blue, orange and green tattoo of a koi fish. Hmmm. This was the sort of receptor nodule that came before Dr. Newburg's subdermal implants. It was an implant, but still required wiring to make the connection. Perhaps this could be an opening for Chickee to have "someone on the inside" who could help her get necessary stuff, like rubbing alcohol and cotton balls.

Gus smiled at her across the table again. This reminded her she was going to determine if he had a receptor as well. Although he didn't seem sickly now, Chickee knew after so long here at Green Valley, a person's health could take a downturn very quickly. You could never predict who or when it would happen to next. She smiled back. She felt a little bit like a detective, and she liked that. Finally, a little excitement in an otherwise drab and boring life.

Life used to be exciting. She spooned a little taste of lemon pudding to see if it was what she wanted, and concentrated inwardly on trying to remember one of the happiest memories of her life. Marrying Jared? Reece's birth? Reece learning to walk?

Traveling to the coast with Sean? She decided to start earlier. The day she taught Barf to shake.

Chickee was ten years old when she got Barf. He was a mutt, but she loved him like he was the most precious and loving dog that ever existed. She brushed his wavy black and white coat daily. She gave him baths as often as he would tolerate them. She taught him in the first week to sit, speak, and wait. It took a little longer to teach him to shake, but it was so worth it. She could show off to Eric, Sherry and Karla how smart her dog was, which by default showed how dumb Eric's lizards, Sherry's gerbil and Karla's bird were. Well, she had to admit, the bird could at least whistle the wolf call. But Barf had *manners*. And she never let her siblings forget it. That was a good day.

She seemed to have day-dreamed the meal away. James was ready to clear plates and she had hardly touched anything besides the pudding. Chickee took a drink of the weak tea then pushed back from the table. She had to figure out a plan to get the supplies she needed.

She went to her room and dug way deep back in the back of the bottom drawer of the dresser. She had to get on her hands and knees to do it, and she still could, but these days she almost always needed help getting back up from the floor. The linking device was in a recycled fiber bag in the back of the bottom drawer. The brown fiber bag crinkled as she reached back there and got hold of it to pull it out. *KROGER* said the recycled bag in red ink on the side. Chickee wondered to herself how long it had been since she had actually set foot inside a grocery store.

After crawling from the dresser to the bed, she put the bag on the bed, then she pulled herself up onto the bed, with a little bit of a struggle. She sat on her bed and uncurled the top of the bag, peeking inside like she was unwrapping a birthday present very cautiously. She reached in and pulled it out. The Velcro was yellowed and stiff, but still seemed to hold tight to itself. She carefully laid out all the wires along the length of the bed next to her, and checked the leads connecting the wrist wrap. She had to adjust her glasses on her nose and balance them just right to be able to see the spot where they connected. Next, she checked the receptor end nodes. Would they work? She didn't really have any of the nifty stickers she always used with it. She hoped maybe a Band-Aid would work if she couldn't get ahold of any EKG stickers. Who was she kidding? Last time she got her insides looked at and listened to, they used this huge computerized machine that did it all: EKG, CAT Scan, MRI. All she had to do was lay as still as possible on the hospital bed. Technology was wonderful when you were the impatient patient, but when you were the old fashioned medical personnel, it really cramped your style.

She heard someone coming up the hallway with loud voices. Very quickly, she stashed the device back into the KROGER sack and crumple rolled the top of it down. It was a mad dash to the dresser to lean down low and stick it back into the bottom drawer, which she had absent mindedly left open. Whew.

"Hey, Chickee, how about a shower here in a sec?" suggested Tara. Chickee smiled and nodded her head without saying anything. "Okay, I'll be back in just a bit." Tara exited as quickly as she came. Bummer, now she would not get to go check on Murphy tonight like she had planned. But a shower would be nice. Nothing like a little water therapy for old creaky bones.

After showers were done, James helped Teresa, the night nurse tuck everyone into bed. She could do most things for herself, but it was nice they still came in and asked if she needed anything. "Hey, James," Chickee was feeling like time was fleeting. It couldn't wait until his next shift. "What's the story behind your koi fish?"

"Huh? Oh, this? Well, I was younger and stupider and dating a gorgeous oriental fairy devil. I got this for her. Ha. Good thing I have a forgiving wife, huh?" he chuckled at himself.

"Hmmm. I noticed one of your fish's scales is shimmery. How did you do that?"

"Oh this?" He pointed to his receptor nodule. "This is something I inherited from another yet younger and stupider event: I was in a serious motorcycle accident."

"Ah. That explains it. How many sessions did you have?"

"Linking? Well, because I was young and stupid, I only did it for two weeks. Long enough to get the implant and then feel like I was too high and mighty for that mental mumbo jumbo. You know about linking?"

"Yes, I was a Linker for several years." That was a nice, vague answer, she felt.

"Cool. Sorry. I've since mended my wicked ways. My daughter needed some help when she smashed her little hand in the airlock door. The Linker helped her so much. But she has a subdermal implant. You like it?"

"What?"

"You like linking? You did it for a while, eh?"

"Yes. It was worth every minute." She didn't explain the double meaning on her comment. Every minute she gained. Every minute she linked with a sick person. Every minute she spent helping people. Every minute her life was lengthened.

"Well, goodnight, Chickee. Sweet dreams."

"Goodnight, kids." At her age, Chickee addressed nearly everyone as "kids."

Chapter Thirty-Eight

Murphy's Transition

2092

His papery thin eyelids showed his eyes moving back and forth in REM sleep. They were talking, or she was at least, a few minutes ago. But Murphy fell in and out of sleep so easily. His thin bony arm moved slightly as he was busy in his dreams accomplishing who knows what kind of work.

"I'm going to hold your hand here, Murphy, and talk to you for a little while." Chickee gently pulled his hand closer to the edge of the bed so she could begin wrapping the wrist band receiver around his forearm. She paid close attention to his breathing. She knew for this adult linking session, he would need to be as calm as possible. She didn't want to ruffle his feathers or do anything to make his paranoia surface, or the attempt to link with him would have to wait for another day.

The EKG badges were nearly impossible to track down without bringing someone else in on her plan. So finally, Friday afternoon, Chickee decided she would have to do a wrist-to-wrist connection by wiring together the two systems she had with her at Green Valley. One was a spandex wrist band, about four inches in length, and fit tightly, snugly on her forearm. Murphy's arms were very slender and seemed so fragile, so she planned to use the spandex for herself and use the adjustable Velcro one for him. She had only done a wrist to wrist connection a few times, with children who had had open heart surgeries or other conditions that made their chest area extremely sensitive.

Murphy turned slightly, pulling his arm away from the edge of the bed where Chickee was sitting. She tried to soothingly rub the inside of his forearm, knowing this would relax him. Once she felt he was not going to turn completely over and pull his arm up close to his body, she brought a couple of cotton balls and the bottle of rubbing alcohol out of her shoulder bag. She wanted to have the best link possible for the attempt, so she had cleaned off the transmitter nodules of the insides of both wrist bands until they shined, and now she needed to make sure his arm was clean and free of any residue or oils that would hinder the connection.

Only once did Murphy seem to pull away from the cool rub of the cotton ball. Chickee was careful to go slow and gentle. A sound in the hallway made her look up momentarily from what she was concentrating on, but she saw it was another resident walking by, heading further down the hallway, mumbling to himself as he went. Next, she placed the Velcro wrist band underneath Murphy's arm, and tightened it up as tight as she could get it without disturbing him. At this point she stopped and composed herself a moment. It had been nearly seven years since she had linked with anyone, young or old. She began breathing very purposefully, very slowly in, pause, then very slowly out again.

"Murphy, you remember how Steven was walking in that field across the bridge? We're going for a little nature walk today, okay? You enjoy yourself and focus on seeing him again. I wish you Godspeed."

Very calmly, with deliberate slowness, almost in a sort of reverence for the moment, not only because this would be a transition from life into afterlife, but also because it had been so long since she linked with somebody, Chickee slid the spandex wrist band over her hand and nudged it securely into place for the best possible link. She felt a need to touch Murphy physically, so she put her other hand on his shoulder; this meant she was leaning over, almost half lying next to him on the bed. With her elbow, she slid the switch on the device to ON. She began to focus on his heartbeat and link her heartbeat to match it. Then she visualized the bridge in her story. The field across the bridge was green and speckled with spring flowers.

Suddenly, she felt Murphy's hand grasp hers—the one nearest his was her linking arm with the wrist band attached, so both of their linking arms were also hand-clasped together. "Let's go," he said calmly. So Chickee continued to visualize the bridge, and walking across it with him. He held her hand all the way. They walked over to the tree where the fishing pole stood leaning against it. "Steven?" Murphy called. The boy was running with the puppy at the far end of the field of grass. Murphy squeezed her hand and smiled. "Steven! Over here!" Then he let go.

"Oh!" It took her by surprise. At the moment he let go of her hand, she felt her heartbeat take a leap. She released her grip on his shoulder, not realizing how tightly she had hold of him. She opened her eyes and tried to sense his heartbeat. It was very faint. Quickly, she disconnected the Velcro wrist band, then the spandex wrist band and stuffed them into her bag. It suddenly occurred to her she would be in a real fix if he died while she was actually hooked up. It all of a sudden seemed extremely urgent that she got herself and her things out of his room.

Another sound in the hallway made her jump up to her feet. She stood still a moment for two reasons. Number one, she wanted to listen if someone was coming. Number two, her head was throbbing so loudly, it made her a little dizzy. *Oh yeah. After-headache.* It had been long enough since her last link up, she had almost forgotten. Holding onto the doorframe, and the railing down the hallway, she edged her way back to her own room, wishing she had thought of sunglasses or a shawl to shade her eyes from the bright fluorescent institutional lights.

After taking a long drink of water at the sink with her glass marked "Michelle Lane," Chickee climbed into bed, stuffed her bag underneath it, and pulled the covers up over her eyes. *Ooooow.* Yes, now she remembered why linking was so excruciatingly painful. But, as she was fading off, she realized something really important: this adult link was not difficult like the others. *Hmmm.* Something to ponder further when she could think straight again.

"Chickee? Chickee? Wake up, honey." In her deep sleep, Chickee thought it was Jared calling her to get up.

"Jared?" she mumbled in a sleepy soft voice. "Come here and hold me."

"Chickee? It's time for dinner." James, the nurse repeated to her. *Oh. Only him.* She was extremely disappointed when she woke up enough to realize when and where she was. "I know. I'm sorry. I wasn't who you were hoping for, eh?"

"No," she said bluntly. "Oooh, I was sleeping so hard!" she groaned.

"Are you hungry? Time to eat, Chickee."

Chapter Thirty-Nine

Bridgette

September 2092

"Chickee, you have a visitor."

As she looked up from her nap, she recognized the red-headed lady right away. "Bridgette! Oh how nice to see you!"

"Hi, Chickee Mom," Bridgette responded with an enthusiastic smile and a hug. Bridgette held a rather large gift bag slung over her arm. The green paisley bag had light green tissue paper fluffing out of the top of it, and a small oval tag hanging down from the shiny green ribbon handles. "Here, I got you a little something. Happy birthday!"

"Oh, thank you, Bridgette! It's a beautiful bag. What in the world could I possibly need?" Chickee peeked into the bag and gently pushed aside the green tissue paper. A brightening smile came over her face when she realized what was inside the bag. "Oh!" she exclaimed. She pulled the gift out of the bag, less gently now in her excitement, and stared with glee at the large framed photo of the three cats lying on the old green couch. "There's Cory, Buster, and Ray. This is so precious. Thank you, Bridgette! How thoughtful!"

"I found the picture on an old memory stick from before I left for college. I knew you would enjoy it."

"Oh, Bridgette, I love it. Thank you! Those three were such buddies; look at how they snuggled up. Of course it wasn't long before that turned into kitty WWW! They loved to wrestle too!"

"Yeah, I remember," chuckled Bridgette. "So how have you been? Are they feeding you enough around here? You look so slim."

"Hey now, let me enjoy this. Could you say that last part again?"

"What? 'You look so slim'?" she questioned.

"Yes! Ah. One more time."

"You-look-so-slim."

"Why, thank you!" Chickee smiled big and bright. "You do realize, or I dunno, maybe you don't know, but all my life, the only skinny part of me was my *feet!* And even then, after I had Reece, pregnancy puffed up my feet to match the rest of my body, so I couldn't even say my feet were slim. It is so nice to hear someone thinks I'm 'slim'."

"Okay, skinny-minny, don't they feed you enough around here?" *Bridgette was such a sight for lonesome eyes,* thought Chickee. They made small talk and caught up on Bridgette's work with Mother's Heartbeat. She was Stella's daughter, and had been trained as a Linker in her late twenties. Stella had groomed her to take over the management of the business; that had happened in 2075. That was after the worst of the hacker problems with Mother's Heartbeat devices, but before the last straw, bringing about Chickee's decision to no longer be a Linker.

Chickee was thinking to herself about revealing her decision to help some of the residents here transition. Bridgette would understand, if anybody would. Her mother was still alive and lived retired on an island in the Caribbean with her rich third husband. After Jared died, Chickee contacted her college boyfriend, Sean, but no matter how long she lived, she always thought surviving one dead husband was enough for her. Stella was always the one who was living life to the fullest, even in her post-centennial years.

Bridgette wore a smart coral pantsuit in the latest style, a style Chickee hardly recognized. She had her beautiful red hair swept up in a large tight bun on top of her head really high, reminding Chickee of a 1970s beehive. She didn't wear a lot of makeup; her skin was naturally beautiful and youthful. Bridgette must've been in her sixties by now, but she certainly didn't look it. She had been linking since she was twenty-eight, so she had kept her youthfulness for a long time.

"Bridgette, I have something to tell you," she started in a low voice, looking cautiously towards the door to her room, "And I don't want you to get mad at me. Or turn me in to the authorities for violating Mother's Heartbeat guidelines. I have an idea I was meant to be here for a specific purpose. There are a lot of hurting people in a nursing home, too, and I can help them. Wait. Don't say anything. I know it's taking a chance to link up with adults. But what have I got to lose? I'm ready to be done. If it saps all the life left out of me like a slow leaking battery, what does it matter to me? I've missed having a purpose, being able to help people. Now I've found a way to *help* them. Whew. That's the most words I've said in a week. But I didn't want you to interrupt me before I got done saying my piece. Now: what do you think?"

"So... Really? You are linking up with old people to help them manage their pain? Why would you do that if it causes you so much pain?" Bridgette was trying to understand.

"No. Not to manage their pain. To help them *transition,*" Chickee explained in a hushed voice. The look on Bridgette's face changed from curious confusion to one of smiling comprehension.

"Chickee," Bridgette's cheerful voice surprised the older woman, "You haven't watched any news in ages, have you?"

"Well, no. I just don't spend time in the common room that much. And I was never fond of spending hours on my PCD like the younger generation. Of course, they don't let us have those anymore here anyway." Her face twisted in a look of frustration at that fact. There were some independences she really missed, like calling Reece whenever she wanted.

"The news about a year ago would've interested you. Chickee, they have legalized elder euthanasia!"

"What?! You're kidding! Oh hmmm." She thought for a moment. "Yes, I was worried I'd be arrested for it, but that changes things a little."

"Well, there are guidelines one must follow, of course, but I have to tell you, Mother's Heartbeat has worked on a few adjustments to the goals and mission statement with this new development as well." She paused meaningfully as she tried to read Chickee's response at absorbing this new information. "I know you comprehend the scope of what I'm saying."

"Hmmmm," Chickee thought some more, and then decided to risk it all. She knew she could trust Bridgette. "I just adjusted two wrist bands to send and receive, customized, like Jared would have done for me if he was here. One spandex, one Velcro. I've already linked with someone. He visualized walking over a bridge and I held his hand along the way. Literally. I think holding his hand while being linked made a difference in how difficult the side effects of adult linking were for me. Do you think it's crazy?"

"Oh yes. It's crazy. I mean, every Linker *tries* linking with an adult. None of us want to see our loved ones suffer. But no one has ever been successful. At least none other than with Brenda back in 2025. But that was *you*, wasn't it? Hmmm."

"Bridgette, please don't share this with anyone. I think it is probably dangerous for you to even know. Can you pretend you don't know, when it's all—over?. Do you think you could do that for me?"

"I'll do my best, Chickee. But I don't think you need to worry about the police coming to arrest you... I wish I could tell Malcolm. He's on another deep sea excursion. You'd never guess the man is in his sixties! I guess being married to me has kept him young." Bridgette smirked and curtsied to the side as if she were on stage, taking credit for a fine performance.

"How is Malcolm? Such a dear man. You could tell him. He can't tell anybody else, though. He wouldn't tell anybody, would he?"

"Nope. He's trustworthy. He's smart. He married me, didn't he?" she joked. "He'll get back from the coast on Tuesday. Did you know Friday is our fortieth anniversary? He promised he would take me on the next trip. But I've got to get Ellie to takeover Mother's Heartbeat stuff first.

"Hey, Chickee Mom, I guess I ought to be going. The afternoon has flown by. It has been so good to visit with you. Now you behave yourself, and *be careful!* You are always thinking of others, but whatever you do, just don't get caught in the room with your device hooked up to a dead person. There are a few *guidelines* you might be smudging in lack of paperwork and so forth." She gathered her coral jacket and took her PCD out of her pocket, checking the time. "I've really got to go. I love you, Chickee Mom. Happy birthday!"

"I love you too, Bridgette. Thanks for the visit."

As Bridgette walked back down the hall to the exit, Chickee's mind took her back to her first glimpse of that bright red hair.

2020

"I have some news for you, Chickee." Stella made a point today to catch her at the hospital before her linking session.

"Hi Stella, what's up?"

"Well, something we never expected to happen. Lee and I are going to have a baby! We are so shocked and pleased. We never imagined we'd have another chance in the twilight years. But it may mean some changes for our scheduling. Do you think I should link only with babies during pregnancy? Is that something I should even be concerned about?"

"Stella, I don't think we should take any chances. Let's be sure you are up for it, especially when the headaches can do you in if you go for too-old of patients. The last thing you'll need while your body is growing a baby is to have those excruciating headaches. We'll talk with Sharon and Olivia. I know they will understand."

So throughout her pregnancy, Stella was the one designated for infant linkings, while the others took any child older than one year. Stella's pregnancy went fairly smoothly except for the gestational diabetes she dealt with.

And then she requested something really unusual. She wanted Chickee to be a Linker present at the birth, in case the baby needed any extra attention. Chickee realized at this point, Stella was afraid of something.

"What is it? Are you okay?"

"Chickee, I don't know why we haven't done it before. Shouldn't a Linker be at every birth? The birth mother is exhausted; many times numb from the epidural. Yes, she is the prenatal heartbeat that baby knows, but when she is needing rest so badly, why not transition a child into *breathing* life with a Linker?"

"Yes, but, surely you do not suggest we implant a child with a receiver as soon as they are born? How difficult will it be to justify with the FDA?"

"Why couldn't we make a tiny wrist receiver? Or go old fashioned and use the EKG badges like in the early days? We would have to use the special paper tape that doesn't harm their tender baby skin, but I don't want to take the chance, to need a Linker there, and not have one."

"I will, of course, be there for you and your baby, Stella, but are you okay? Are you worried about something?"

"Well," Stella started, "I'm just so old and tired. I know women have healthy babies well into their forties these days, but *technically* I am fifty-four years old, no matter what benefits I've had from linking. That scares me."

Of course Stella grew very tired, especially by the seventh month. She asked to take fewer linking sessions altogether. She was beginning to feel urgent about nesting, but it was too soon. She had set up her midwife and hospital back up plan by month four, so everything seemed in order when she went into labor at week 33. A little too early to risk being at home for the baby's sake, she went to the back-up plan revised, which had her midwife at the hospital delivery room.

Bridgette came into the world almost seven weeks early, but she didn't seem like a premature baby because the first thing anybody noticed about her was her bright red hair, and lots of it, sticking up in every direction. She seemed strong and determined, right from the start. At least everybody thought so.

"Oh, you are so beautiful, little girl. What will your name be?" Chickee was second only to Stella and Lee in getting to hold the little bundle after the nurses had cleaned her and wrapped her up in a soft pink receiving blanket.

"Bridgette Elaine," mumbled a very tired Stella.

"Hello, Bridgette Elaine," Chickee continued cooing to her, "You are a very lucky little girl. Yes, you are. Your mama and daddy will take such good care of y--" Suddenly, Chickee got really quiet. "Wait. Bridgette? Hey." She patted Bridgette's little back rather firmly. "Nurse? She's stopped breathing! Quick!" The nurse immediately came and flipped the tiny baby over on her tummy in one hand, and patted her back with the other. With a cough and a wail, little Bridgette sucked in air again and started howling.

Everyone left in the room was on pins and needles. The nurse had rushed Bridgette to the newborn immediate care room next door and the doctors were busy doing all sorts of tests to make sure the cessation of breathing wasn't going to happen again. Chickee was anxious to get in there and have some linking contact with her. Stella was upset and crying. She couldn't gather herself together.

"I'm going to go in there," determined Chickee. She had already prepped her wristband on her own arm, and had small strips of paper tape on the EKG badge ready to place it on Bridgette's tiny chest for linking. As soon as a nurse opened the door, she rushed in despite protests from the nurse. Stella was pleading with the nurse to let her in there to link with the baby.

Bridgette seemed to be stable and calmer now, although her little face matched her bright red hair because she had been crying and stressed from all the doctors and nurses' poking and pricking. With the damp cotton ball she had in her left hand, Chickee swiped a spot just below Bridgette's left collar bone, and fanned it a second to dry. She taped the EKG badge snugly to Bridgette's chest in the same spot, turned her device on, calming her thoughts to a hum of a children's lullaby as she captured the baby's quick heartbeat and linked her own to a familiar beat of swish saa swish, swish saa swish. The expression on the baby's face calmed and her breathing evened out. Chickee softly hummed to Bridgette as she picked her back up, cradled her in her arms, and focused on the linking.

To the tune of "Rock-A-Bye Baby," she sung to Bridgette softly. "My dear, my Bridgette, safe in my arms. You can rest easy, Mommy is near. Welcome to this world, welcome to life. You are such a sweetie; your red hair's so nice." She didn't usually sing to her patients, but this one seemed so special. She fell in love with the little one as she made up the words to the familiar tune. "Dearest little Bridgette, you can rest easy now. Just lay here in my arms and draw strength somehow. Your precious breathing, something so new. Just breathe in and breathe out, you know I love you." Chickee stared wonderingly at her dark red tiny eyelashes as Bridgette's eyes got heavy and they fluttered gradually to her cheeks.

How could this be? She was so immediately taken with this little baby girl. She shared a special bond with Bridgette, and now her heartstrings were all tied up. And it didn't end there.

Long after that day in spring, Chickee was an integral part of Bridgette's life. As Bridgette crawled, then toddled, Stella graciously shared the milestone moments with Chickee, making sure she was there for the first steps, the first birthday with cake all over her face, and many other tiny moments that made her smile when she thought of them.

When Bridgette started talking, she called her "Chickee Mom," and it stuck.

Chapter Forty

A Wedding

2092

From all the décor around the nursing home, residents guessed what season it was. Twinkle lights and red ribbons around the windows in the dining area, and a tiny plastic tinsel tree on the counter at the main nurses' station. Of course the influx of caroling groups attempted to put everyone in a jovial holiday mood as well.

2052

The holiday décor reminded Chickee of Bridgette and Malcolm's beautiful wedding. Bridgette was twenty-seven and had completed her Linker training. Malcolm was establishing himself as a medical research intern at the University. They dated for two and a half years before he finally proposed.

Bridgette had always wanted a holiday wedding, with the dark green holly, the red ribbons and the smell of pine and cinnamon in the air. She made her Chickee Mom a part of the ceremony by having her bring the flask of gold sand to the unity table. Stella brought the flask of white sand, and Malcolm's stepmother brought the jar with red sand. Instead of a unity candle during that part of the ceremony, Malcolm and Bridgette each took turns pouring in the different colors of sand, making a beautiful new design as "the two become one," combining all the colors of their wedding into a unique "unity jar" that would never melt or become disfigured like so many unity candles had done over the years. It was beautifully symbolic, and Chickee felt honored to be a part of it.

Weddings always reminded Chickee of her own wedding day. She sat in the audience with her hands clasped in her lap, pretending Jared was there holding her hands in spirit as they remembered their own wedding day in 2007. Sometimes events like these were full of mixed emotions because she knew she should be so happy for Bridgette and Malcolm, yet it was inwardly poignantly sad, because her longing for Jared was renewed all over again.

Back in present day, Chickee realized she sat in the gathering room with tears rolling down her face. Gratefully, no one noticed. They were all in their own thoughts, or trying to follow the mystery show on the television. With a big sigh, she stood up from her chair and walked down the hall to have a look at the lone tree in the field outside the west window. It was December and the branches looked naked without any leaves on them. Chickee saw a Cardinal pause briefly on one of the lower branches. Its bright red feathers were much like the Christmas red of Bridgette's wedding. With another sigh, she headed back to her own room.

Chapter Forty-One

Making a Difference

February 2093

Chickee didn't do many transition linkings at the nursing home too closely together or someone would figure out what was happening. She had to be so careful. She spaced them out with a random number of days or weeks in between so it didn't seem like a pattern of deaths.

So far, Murphy transitioned to the grassy field with his little brother; Dina, who carried her purse with a teddy bear sticking out of it (until she couldn't walk anymore) had "gone to Paris with her sister;" Sal, who spent so long in a reclining hover bed, slurping all his meals through a straw till he was too weak to do even that, gratefully accepted Chickee's offer of a restful, painless sleep, and Grumpy Pete, who declined in health so typically over the last several months since she first had the idea of transition linking, and who took every ounce of strength Chickee had to get him to focus and breathe, had finally followed the little white dog into the tunnel.

Her own health visibly declined as well. Nurses commented in hushed tones when they thought Chickee wasn't listening about how much her skin had aged lately, as well as about her significant loss of strength and endurance to walk around and talk to everyone in the wing.

She was barely able to make it back to her own room and her own bed after the transition linking for Grumpy Pete. She anticipated his transition would be more stressful on her, though, because of the nature of his mental health. She didn't back down from it. He seemed receptive to the idea of Chickee taking the pain away by linking. He was clearly miserable without the basic abilities and strength to be independent. He resented needing help to go to the toilet; he made it difficult for the nurses to deal with him. Chickee actually did more than one linking session with him, to show him it would be okay, if he let her help him. This really took its toll on her. The staff thought she had caught a flu for the two days she lay in bed and moaned with fever and headache and chills as she recovered from that first link up with Grumpy Pete. Only she knew the way she felt was all due to her daring to link up with an angry, mentally ill adult.

It was during her recovery from the final link up with Grumpy Pete that Bridgette came for another visit. Chickee visibly ached with the after-headache, and Bridgette in her Mother's Heartbeat experience recognized this right away.

"Oh, Chickee Mom, you're doing it, aren't you?" she asked with a look of concern on her face. She reached out for a gentle hug, recognizing how frail Chickee had become since she last saw her.

"This one was the most difficult yet. I won't do anymore that are so difficult. In fact, I may only have one more left in me. I guess it's having its desired effect, huh? I'm tired, Bridgette. A hundred twenty-one years is a good, long life, don't you think?"

"That makes me *not* want to tell you what Mother is doing. She has decided to open up a little snow cone stand there on St. John's Island, because she's 'bored'. I'm about ready to pass the baton to Ellie with Mother's Heartbeat. She is ready. She has been training in the scheduling and communications aspects for a few months now. I'm really proud of her ambition. Maybe I'll go help Mom run her snow cone stand in the Coral Bay, hahaha."

"I already have a person in mind to help for the next transition. It'll be about three weeks before I'll be able to do anything though. So far no one has made any connection to me. I'm glad I could help them."

"Please be careful, Chickee Mom. Here, I actually came to bring you something. A little bit of security. Based on our last conversation, I drew up some papers that would arbitrarily help you 'follow the guidelines' in your efforts. Sign by the little yellow tabs; I think there are five places for your signature. I figured paper and pen would be easiest for you. I can scan these in for the electronic records."

Chickee was grateful, but too tired to worry about technicalities at this moment, so she perfunctorily signed her name on each line and gave the papers back to Bridgette.

"Okay. Sorry it's such a short visit, I've got to run, dear. Love you, Chickee Mom."

"Love you too, sweetie. Take care."

"Bye." And she walked out the door and down the hall.

Chapter Forty-Two

No More Fear

March 2093

A couple of weeks went by and Chickee attempted to talk some more with Darlene. Except for the times when she expressed distaste for her liquid meals, or when she talked about being afraid, Darlene didn't say much. She seemed to appreciate Chickee's company, though, so sometimes the ladies would spend time together looking out the window at the end of the hallway, Chickee grasping the bar along the wall, as her legs seemed weaker underneath her than she ever remembered, and Darlene in her hover bed turned sideways so she could look out over the field and the lone tree that her friend liked so well. Sometimes she would talk about the different birds she saw out there, and other times, they would watch the wind blow the dried leaves around on the ground.

She used these moments to reassure Darlene there was nothing to be afraid of. Chickee knew linking with someone who was full of fear would be a miserably painful experience for her as the Linker. She wanted Darlene to feel calm and ready to transition when the time came. In rare moments, Darlene shared details about herself and Chickee tucked away to use during linking. She learned that Darlene had two babies who had died right after childbirth because Darlene had been doing drugs. She learned that Darlene had served six years in jail, plus three years of community service for her involvement in drugs. Most significantly, she learned that Darlene had a nodule implant. Darlene told her about the meningitis she had as a child, and how a Linker helped her recover more quickly.

Once she had that piece of information, she prepared the device by removing the Velcro wrist band on the receiver end, and cleaning off the tip of the wire that would hook into the nodule receiver just below Darlene's collar bone.

She watched Darlene carefully. She recognized the signs of excessive tiredness and lack of speech as Darlene slipped further from any quality of life. When the day came that Darlene was unable to maneuver her hover bed out of their bedroom, Chickee knew time was close.

She ate her lunch thoughtfully. The staff thought she was brooding today because she was so silent. This was a yellow lunch—a grilled cheese sandwich with yellow slice cheese, pineapple chunks in a little Styrofoam cup, and vanilla pudding in a Styrofoam cup. Chickee actually wasn't hungry at all, but she was thinking about linking up later that evening, and the strength she would need to make it back to her own bed afterward. So she ate part of her sandwich and spooned out the vanilla pudding bite by bite.

It was difficult for her to bend down and pull the KROGER bag out from the back of the bottom drawer of the dresser this time. She sat one last time on her bed, with the door to her room closed, and the privacy curtain pulled, just in case, and checked all the parts and connections of the device diligently. Satisfied that it was going to serve its purpose for this linking with Darlene, she tucked it all back into the sack, put it under the top cover of her bed near the pillow, then sat in the easy chair and took a snooze. She dreamt of a carnival, with a roller coaster and a Ferris wheel and a colorful animal carousel. In her dream, a young Jared got on the Ferris wheel with a smile, and whirled around and around blissfully. As the Ferris wheel slowed down to load and unload passengers, Jared ended up waiting at the top. But when his cart rolled down to ground level, he wasn't in it. Chickee woke up.

Chickee awoke to find her dinner tray left for her on the side table, because she had snoozed right through the evening meal. Oh dear. She figured on linking with Darlene this evening. She wondered if the nurses had already prepped Darlene for bedtime. She pulled back the privacy curtain to find Darlene wasn't in the room, so she decided she would casually go see what was going on at the nurses' station.

First, she drank her tea in one long gulp. She knew she would be so thirsty later. Then she checked the KROGER sack under her pillow. It was still there, so she walked out to see what was going on. The nurses were finishing up shower time for a couple of residents, and the nurses' station was quiet. No conversations meant she couldn't get much indication of how Darlene might be tonight. She decided to find Darlene and see for herself.

Chickee found her roommate in Jerilyn's room, and they were watching a very loud TV. "Hello?" she tested. "It's me, Chickee."

"Yeah, come in," said Jerilyn. When she looked, Darlene's hoverbed was turned so she could see the TV, but Darlene's eyes were closed. Maybe she would be willing to go back to their room since she was snoozing through the show anyway.

"Hi, Jerilyn. I came to find Darlene. Has she been snoozing long?"

"I dunno. A while." *Hmmm.* Chickee wondered if she should bring Darlene back to their room.

As Jerilyn refocused her attention on the loud TV, she walked over to Darlene's hoverbed. "I'm gonna take her back to her room now."

"Oh. Mmm," she seemed to be a woman of few words tonight.

Chickee walked around to the other end of Darlene's hover bed. "Hi, girl. So, how you doin' tonight?" Darlene was very relaxed. She looked at Chickee, but didn't say anything at all. Chickee didn't wait for a response. She pressed the release button for the brake and started pushing Darlene down the hall before she continued, under her breath, "Remember how I talked about helping you sometime? Do you want to have a really good sleep tonight?"

Once again, Darlene looked at her, but didn't say anything. Chickee waited to get a ways down the hall before she continued. "I can use your implant to help you. I have a linking device. Do you want to try it?" she asked, very close to Darlene's ear. Chickee turned the corner around the nurses' station and continued towards the door to the room they shared.

Darlene continued to look intently at Chickee. It seemed as though she could not get words to come to her mouth tonight. "That's okay, Darlene. Just blink once for yes, twice for no. Are you willing to give it a try?" she asked softly. Darlene slowly blinked once, and smiled a half a smile at Chickee. It seemed the other half of her face was not responding. "Okay. Here, let me get us inside the room."

As Chickee put her sleeve snugly on her left arm, she talked to Darlene. "Have you ever been on a hover train? I used to love the speed and the rush. Maybe we could take a train ride tonight. What do you think?" Darlene slowly blinked once, and attempted to revisit a half smile for Chickee.

Chickee found Darlene's implant nodule directly below her left collarbone, and had to slough off some skin that had grown over the receptor with a little piece of pumice stone she had in her own things. Darlene frowned as she did this. "Yes, I know. I'm sorry. I have to expose the nodule. Are you ready? Wait. Let me shut the door." She walked around the privacy curtain and clicked the door shut. She walked back around and sat on the chair next to Darlene's hover bed. She reset the bed to hover very low to the ground, to reduce chances of a fall, if she was to roll out of bed. Chickee leaned over, hooked up the wire to Darlene's receptor, and put her right hand on Darlene's left shoulder.

"Do you want to hold my hand?" she asked. Darlene had trouble reaching up high enough to hold her hand, so Chickee scooted down toward the middle of the bed. She rested her left arm on the edge of the bed, and held Darlene's right hand across her belly. The covers were up tight under Darlene's flabby arms. "Now, just relax. Breathe easy. Think about happy things. We're gonna have a thrill riding on the hover train tonight."

Darlene followed Chickee's instructions with full trust and interest. She was surprised at how simple this transition linking was. Soon they both had eyes closed, and she visualized both of them walking towards the train with Darlene holding her hand. Darlene smiled a full smile and was visibly excited to get on the train. As Chickee began to step up onto the train with her, Darlene held up a hand for her to "stop." With both her hands, she held Chickee's hand, then brought it up to her lips and kissed it. She pushed Chickee away from the door of the train and smiled again. As the alert was sounded for departure, Darlene made a sign language gesture to Chickee, her flat palm at her chin, then moving down and away from her face into an open palm. "Thank you," it meant. Chickee smiled back at her and stepped back from the train.

"You're welcome, my friend. Safe travels, Darlene," Chickee said to her.

So quickly it was over. Darlene had understood completely, and was ready for the journey. As Chickee opened her eyes, she felt Darlene's grasp on her hand relax, and she knew the time was close. Fighting through her weakness and after-headache, she disconnected from Darlene's implant nodule and slipped the sleeve off her left arm. She stuffed the device into the bag and slowly pushed the privacy curtain back, making her way back to her own bed.

At the sink, she drank with a cupped hand, big slurps of water, until she had it running all the way to her elbows. She didn't think she could bend down to the bottom drawer, so she stuffed the KROGER bag into the top drawer of her bedside table as best she could, and crawled under the covers fully dressed, aching to put her body to rest.

Chapter Forty-Three

How Dare You Steal My Joy

2024

Chickee and Jared set the sprinkler out in the back yard for Reece to run through. It was such a hot summer. Jared blended up some strawberry smoothies for all three of them, and they were laughing, laughing, laughing. Such a good feeling to be so carefree and laugh with your head flung back in glee.

Reece thought the sprinkler was so much fun he was going to get the cats in on the fun. Despite the protests and warnings of his parents, Reece was determined that the cats should play in the sprinkler with him. Buster was the victim of the moment. He was very tolerant of Reece's antics, and was one of the best about playing along when Reece wanted to pretend, but he was having nothing of this water flying everywhere!

Soon laughing out loud at the skinny, soaked cat turned to muffled giggles and feigned sympathy as Reece boo-hooed over his scratched arms. Buster jumped with claws extended out of his arms and left several striped welts on the little boy's arms. The need for soothing was momentary though, because he couldn't be bothered with Band-Aids—they would get wet. Soon he was back out romping around under the spray of water, and everyone laughed again and felt the cool spray of water.

Then Chickee looked over at the back gate of the yard. Standing there was a big bulky man with an evil grin on his face. He laughed at Reece's play in the water as well. *How dare he!* She no longer laughed. And when she looked beside her, there was no Jared. *Wait! This is all wrong!*

Suddenly she was tied up and gagged, and walking all around her on the floor were pitifully soaked cats yowling like they're dying slowly. *How could you?! This isn't right! How dare you steal my joy!*

Chickee awoke in her room at Green Valley with the sheets tangled all about her. She was sweating and sobbing. Her head was roaring and pounding with an unbelievable throb. She was so dizzy she felt like she was going to be sick. Weakly, she reached for the button to call a nurse. She was afraid she had wet herself this time.

Chapter Forty-Four

Finally Old

2093

It had been three days since the transition linking session with Darlene. Chickee was awake long enough to hear the staff talking about Darlene passing in the night, and how they were happy for her because she didn't have to be scared anymore.

But they were equally concerned for Chickee, because she hadn't hardly gotten out of bed in the last few days. When she barely woke up the second day, they called the two contact numbers in her file. The first one was actually Bridgette, because she could reach the nursing home sooner than Reece, who was now in Virginia.

The second number was Reece. He was surprised to hear she was so frail, because last time he had seen her at Christmas, she seemed well and rather energetic, especially compared to the other residents. He made arrangements right away to fly out to St Louis and rent a car. Then Reece called the main Mother's Heartbeat number and let Bridgette know he was coming.

They talked briefly about the downturn Chickee had taken recently, and of course Bridgette kept the confidence that Chickee had placed in her and never gave even a hint she knew *why* Chickee had gone on such a quick decline. Instead, she told him about her most recent visit about three weeks ago, and how she had noticed a change in Chickee, especially in her skin and eyes, and in her strength for ordinary actions, like walking down the hall to dinner.

He told Bridgette he planned to arrive on the next day and he would visit the nursing home in the evening after he got into town.

Bridgette told him about her travel plans, too. "I'll be traveling tomorrow as well. To the Caribbean, to visit Mom. She's going to open a snow cone cart at the beach. Crazy, huh? Bad timing, though, considering the downturn Chickee Mom has taken. Ellie has taken over the main responsibilities here, so this is my first vacation in several years."

"Well, have a wonderful trip. Don't worry about Mom. You know she's a strong one. I'll call Ellie and speak to her after my visit with Mom tomorrow night, and then she can update you."

Bridgette and Reece had known each other since they were young. They were more like brother and sister than anything else. Reece was five years old when Bridgette was born, and she and his mom had always shared a special bond. So Bridgette was often over for a baking afternoon, or to get help on sewing her Easter dress. She got her sewing skills from Chickee. Reece did not mind sharing his mother; he was rather used to it with her so busy linking in the early years, and always busy running the business side of Mother's Heartbeat.

"Well, take care. Travel safely, Reece."

"Yes, you do the same. Tell your mom hello. Thanks, Bridgette. Goodnight."

"Goodnight." Bridgette debated over changing her travel plans, but she knew Chickee would have allowed no such thing. Chickee understood how much Mother's Heartbeat could consume a person's time, and she would want Bridgette to take this trip.

Chapter Forty-Five

Reece's Visit

March 2093

When Reece arrived at Green Valley Nursing Center the next evening, the staff seemed wary of him. They expressed their concern for Chickee to him, and told him she had not eaten much of her dinner. They also said she did not get up today at all, and was now in adult diapers. He could tell they were worried he would be angry at them for her condition, but he thanked them and walked down the hall to her room.

"Hi, Mom. It's me, Reece," he walked in the door. *Thankfully,* he thought to himself, *her roommate's bed is empty, so we can have an uninterrupted visit.*

"Hi, Reece. Oh my dear, I must be dying. Since when do you come visit me in the middle of March? It is March, isn't it?"

"Well, Mom. The nurses said you haven't been out of bed much lately. I was worried about you. How are you? Are you able to walk at all?"

"I dunno. I haven't tried. I'm so tired. Just tired. Guess I'm finally feeling my years, hon."

"Yeah, you've been doing so well for so long; I didn't expect you to ever get old, I guess. Are you hungry, Mom? The nurses said you hadn't eaten much today."

"No, not so hungry today. Just tired."

"Did you know Bridgette is traveling to the Caribbean to visit Stella? Ellie has taken over Mother's Heartbeat." A silent pause followed this comment. "Yeah, you seem tired. More tired than I ever remember. Are you hurting?"

"Well, it's like I've got an after-headache that won't go away. Usually sleep will make such a headache subside. But not this one. Like I said, my age is finally catching up to me."

"Mom, do you want me to get you some pain killers? You probably need to drink more, too. 'Headaches are so thirsty,' you always told me. Are you thirsty?"

"Yes, thirsty. And I could take some Tylenol. I could try something to ease this headache. Did you say Bridgette's gone to see Stella?"

"Yes, she turned the management of Mother's Heartbeat over to Ellie."

Chickee took a long swig of the water from her insulated cup with a straw. All the residents had one of these with their names written on them in dark permanent ink by a person who doesn't pay attention to capital letters. To Chickee, her cup looked like it needed editing. MiCheLLe LaNE. A jumbled mixture of small letters and capitals, like a person couldn't make up their mind. She took another long pull of water with the straw and sighed really big afterwards.

"Now, Reece, you know I've made all my arrangements and they're in the lock box at the office."

"Mom, don't talk like that. You can rest up, and feel better tomorrow."

"No, Reece. I've rested up for three days straight and I'm not feeling any more rested than I did when I lay down three days ago. The only kind of resting I'll be doing soon is the eternal kind. And I want you to be ready."

"Yes, Mom, but I've gotten used to having you around. I've been so lucky to have you twice as long as most people get to have their moms. I'm not ready to let you go."

"I know, son. We are never ready to say goodbye to those we love. But I'm looking forward to seeing your father again. Remember I love you, Reece."

"I love you, Mom. You're a great mom. You've helped so many people over the years, and you've given of yourself, even when you knew how it was going to hurt you. I've always been proud of the way you've helped so many people."

"Reece, you're a son to be proud of. Although I had always hoped you'd find a girl; I know it must've been lonely for you at times, but I've very proud of you and your success. I know your father would be proud."

"Well, Lord knows I won't be living as long as you. I'm already seventy-seven, you know. Who knows how many years I've got in me before I get to see you and Dad again."

"What a happy day that will be, Reece. I love you, Son."

"I love you too, Mom. You try to rest now. You look very tired. I'll sit here till you fall asleep."

"Thank you, Reece. I'm so glad you came."

"Me too, Mom. Me, too." He sat there and thought about all sorts of memories of his mom as she started to breathe more slowly. He kissed her on the forehead and walked out. The faces of the staff all looked sorry in already sympathetic smiles. He thanked them again and left to his hotel for the night.

Chapter Forty-Six

The Ferris Wheel

March 2093

The next day Chickee didn't eat hardly anything at breakfast. She didn't feel like lifting it to her mouth. But she was happy. She'd had a nice talk with Reece. She had helped several of her friends from here at Green Valley make the transition, and that gave her much satisfaction. She felt like she had made a choice when she would decline, and that pleased her immensely, too, as if she had beat old age to the punch and not let it decide for her.

Now she needed to wait for her body to give out. She closed her eyes and willed her heart to quit beating. But it wouldn't. She willed her head to split open with the pain of the headache (the painkiller Reece had given her last night had long worn off.) No luck. She held her breath as long as she could and tried to not breathe anymore. That didn't work either. For feeling so old and worn out, she was surprised at her body's determination to continue. She closed her eyes again and tried to slow down her heartbeat to a stop, much like the focused work of linking. But she couldn't slow it down enough. She guessed the brain power it took to concentrate on it required her heart to keep beating. She was between a rock and hard place on this.

She closed her eyes in exasperation then suddenly opened them when there was a soft knock on the door.

"Chickee?" a new young voice inquired.

"Yes?" Her raspy voice surprised her. *My word, how* old *I sound!*

"Hi, I'm Kathryn. Bridgette's my grandma. I just finished advanced Linker training a few months ago. Grandma sent me to you. Are you all packed and ready to go? She said you would be."

She was very young and upbeat and friendly. Chickee liked her instantly, but was a little confused.

"All packed? I didn't know I was supposed to pack a bag..."

"Oh, just a figure of speech. I can tell: you're ready." She smiled really big and continued in her quick efficient manner. Kathryn's spikey short pixie haircut reminded Chickee of her long-ago friend Joan, and she liked her even more for it. "Now, Grandma gave me your linking code, but she also said you're a die hard for the old style. Which would you prefer?"

"Wh-what? You mean you're here to be *my* transition link up? Oh!" Chickee suddenly started to cry.

"Oh wait, don't cry. It's going to be all right. Piece of cake, really," Kathryn consoled.

"Oh, no—it's not that. I'm just so *relieved!* Leave it to my sweet Bridgette to think of everything!" Chickee sat thoughtfully smiling to herself, happy tears still leaking out of the corners of her eyes. Then, realizing what this meant for Kathryn, she protested. "But wait. You can't do this. I will not steal your youth from you. This will be too difficult for you!"

"Chickee, we've got that all worked out. You've done some research of your own over the years, but in the last several years, we've done some research of our own, too. The law changing last year made things a lot easier for us in this regard. I will live a normal life, counter transitions with baby linkings, and even out in the end. Don't you worry about me."

"Oh." Chickee was very tired. She was grateful Bridgette had thought to help her out.

"So: where's your dinosaur device, then? I can use it, if you wish." Chickee pointed to the top drawer near the bed, where she had stashed it before she collapsed into bed a few days ago after linking with Darlene.

"I wanna go to the carnival, okay?" Chickee announced suddenly. "Jared was at the carnival—on the Ferris wheel—a few days ago, in my dream."

"Okay. I love carnivals. Let's get ready to go to the carnival. I'll wear the sleeve, if you'll put on this Velcro wrist band here." She quickly wiped clean and connected the wire that had been hooked to Darlene's nodule implant, then handed the wrist band to Chickee.

"This shall be interesting. I've never been on the receiving end before."

"Oh, it'll be wonderful! It's just what you need. Grandma said you were ready. Are you ready?" Kathryn checked again, looking deep into Chickee's eyes.

"Yes, I think so," she said decisively. "I tried on my own will, but it didn't work. So you can hold my hand 'til we get there, can't you?"

"That's why I'm here," Kathryn replied cheerfully.

"Okay. I'm ready—and Kathryn?"

"Yes, Chickee?"

"Thank you, dear one."

"You're very welcome. Let's go to the carnival, shall we?"

"We shall," Chickee smiled. Then she shut her eyes, allowed herself to relax, and tried to concentrate on her heartbeat.

"Let *me* do the work, okay, Chickee? You rest and relax. You'll sense my hand when we're ready to go."

"Okay." She tried to relax. She allowed herself to feel the immense tiredness that had been overwhelming her for the past week, and then suddenly, there was Kathryn, holding her hand.

And they were walking through the carnival. Kathryn and Chickee walked along, smelling the smells, seeing the twinkling lights and the crowded booths of games. They made a beeline for the Ferris wheel.

Suddenly they were there. And there was Jared. He held the gate open for her to walk through to the seat he'd saved for her. He looked young and vibrant, and oh! How she had missed him!

Chickee squeezed Kathryn's hand, and smiled a thank you as she let go. She walked through the gate and sat down in the cart. Jared sat next to her and grabbed her hand with both of his. He didn't talk; he just smiled and looked deeply into her eyes. She drank in the look of him, knowing she had missed him more than she even realized. He pulled the bar across their laps and latched them in. Soon the ride started to move. With her free hand, Chickee waved goodbye to Kathryn, but she didn't see her anywhere. No matter. Here was Jared. At last. She had so much she wanted to say to him. But when she started to speak, he put his finger over her lips and whispered, "Shhhhh."

He smiled again, and the ride began slowly to move round and round. Then faster still, and Chickee saw the lights all around the carnival were a blur of colors and brightness.

She felt light. Round and round they went. All at once, she noticed they were above the Ferris wheel. Chickee tilted her head back in glee and laughed out loud. Suddenly she was young again like he was. He was still holding her hand and smiling as they went up up up, until they weren't really anywhere and they weren't really anything. But he still held her hand, she knew, and he still smiled and gazed into her eyes. She sensed he was as glad to see her as she was him. Finally, she couldn't hold it in anymore; she felt like she'd been holding her breath and it came out in a rush, "Oh, Jared, I've missed you so much!"

Chapter Forty-Seven

A Mother's Heartbeat

2093

Reece made arrangements based on the instructions he received from the lock box, with the help of Ellie. Since Bridgette was off traveling in the Caribbean this week, the only adjustment he made to Chickee's instructions was that he delayed the memorial service until Bridgette would be back. And she was bringing Stella for the funeral. That was significant. Only one lifelong friend of Chickee's would be there. Everyone else at the funeral would be at least twenty to forty or more years younger than she. He set everything up, the way she had laid it out to be, and the final words of her will were to be read at the memorial service. He decided to ask Kathryn to read it to the gathering.

"An idea born from prenatal memory
that will help many lifetimes of people
Gave me a double lifetime of helping others.
Mother's Heartbeat was a lifeline for me,
even through the heartaches, the headaches, and
     the heartbreaks.
Heartbeat to heartbeat,
We help one at a time:
Focus, Relax, Heartbeat.
It has been my life's honor
To link, to train, to help heal.
And now weightless, my heart will float
Up to those I've missed so much.
Turn your hearts to the world
Focus, Relax, Heartbeat.
Link, Train, Heal
Then float, weightless and free,
Knowing you have helped a double lifetime of
     people.
Never lose the Mother's Heartbeat beating inside
     of you."

And Reece, know that you have always been the inspiration for the beating of MY heart.

The End

About the Author

Kathy Armstrong Pudil is a native New Mexican who was transplanted to Missouri for twenty-four years, and is now living back in the desert. She enjoys reading, writing, cooking, crafts, camping and all things cats. As a writer, Kathy has always kept journals, notes, lists, and written down her dreams in the middle of the night, in hopes of one day publishing a story that's worthy of reading and engrossing to her reader. She lives in New Mexico with her husband and six "kid-ties."

You can contact Kathy at kathyarmstrongpudil@gmail.com
You can read her blog Hearts of Eternity at
http://heartofeternity394938455.wordpress.com